HIS FORBIDDEN DESIRE

THE ISLAND OF YS SERIES

KATEE ROBERT

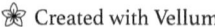 Created with Vellum

For everyone who loves seeing side characters get their HEA
No side character left behind!

ALSO BY KATEE ROBERT

Other Books

TRIGGER WARNING

This book contains characters with a history of childhood abuse (that is *not* described in graphic detail in the story), violence, and the threat of sexual assault.

It also contains jungle sex, really intense beach PDA, and a ridiculously overprotective crankypants hero.

1

———

Princess Camilla Fitzcharles stepped off the helicopter and lifted her hand to shield her eyes. Even with the sun glaring overhead and her stomach tied in knots, she couldn't deny the truth.

She'd arrived in paradise.

The island stretched out before her in a gentle incline that rose to kiss the sky. Merry lights twinkled from a board-walk that stretched the entire length of the bay she'd just landed in, creating a path from Pleasure to Pain, the two main entertainment facilities the Island of Ys offered. They promised to fulfill any fantasy a person could dream up.

Cami wasn't here for either of them.

She had bigger game in mind.

A white woman walked up as the helicopter's blades slowed to stillness, and even though she'd expected a welcome party, it was everything Cami could do not to stare. The blonde wore a fitted dress that showed off an athlete's muscled body and full breasts, sheer black tights, and heels that had to be at least six inches. More than her clothing, the thing that caught Cami's attention was the way she carried herself. This woman was beautiful and powerful and totally secure in that knowledge.

Cami envied her.

The woman stopped in front of her and gave her a shrewd look. "Princess Camilla Fitzcharles. If I had any honor left, I'd send you home with your tail between your legs. This is no place for little girls playing dress up."

If Cami was a different person, she'd shrink down to nothing in the face of such a direct indication of how this woman found her lacking. How *everyone* found her lacking. She wasn't a different person, though. She was a princess, and she'd been taught from birth to brazen her way through situations that made her uncomfortable. She raised her brows. "If you really believe that, then why was I invited?"

"Invited, little princess?" Her red lips quirked into something almost a smile, though the expression didn't reach her amber eyes. "You *weren't* invited. You bribed your way in here." She propped a hand on her hip. "I still wouldn't have let you in, no matter how expensive the price tag, but Death answers to no one. The rest of us just dance to the tune she sets."

Death.

The woman behind the curtain.

Cami had only participated in one conversation with her, and it was more than enough. She was as cold as this one fiery, and she scared the hell out of Cami.

Not enough to make her back off, though.

Nothing would scare her enough for that.

She closed the distance between her and the blonde and lifted her chin. "If you're not going to stop me, then get out of my way."

The woman whistled under her breath. "Little princess has some claws. I like it." She gave Cami another once-over, though this one felt completely different. Just like that, her bristling almost-anger was gone, replaced by merry cheer. She grinned, revealing straight white teeth. "In fact, you're kind of cute in that whole untouched kind of way. Makes me want to do a whole lot of touching."

Cami blinked. "Um, thanks?"

"I know. You're dazzled by my beauty. Don't worry. It happens to everyone." She linked her arm through Cami's and towed her down the steps from the landing pad to a paved walkway that led farther inland. "Welcome to the Island of Ys, where all your dreams and darkest fantasies are possible. For the right price, of course. Since you're here for the Wild Hunt, I expect you'll keep up with the virtuous thing instead of playing with us. A shame."

"When does it start?"

She gave a put-upon sigh. "You know what they say about all work and no play." When Cami just stared, she finally relented. "Three days."

Three days? She might expire from nerves in the meantime. "Why so long to wait?"

The woman laughed. "You have somewhere better to be?" She bumped her shoulder against Cami's. "The island can be ... disconcerting. We like to get everyone together and settled before the game begins." She lowered her voice. "It also lets you get a good look at the competition, which is an asset."

Ah. Of course. She should have thought of that, would have if she wasn't so off balance. "I see."

"There are only three women this year, including you. But I'm getting ahead of myself." Another of those infectious laughs. "I'll show you to your rooms, and you have free rein of the casino floor until dinner tonight. It's an obligatory event, black tie required. All the Wild Hunt events will be held in Pleasure, though you're more than welcome to meander down to Pain as it strikes your fancy."

"I won't be doing that."

"Probably smart of you. Pain has a way of pulling you in." She grinned, merry and bright, and as dangerous as a flame.

The rest of the walk passed in a blur of lights and colors and sounds. Even though they didn't go into the casino called Pleasure itself, moving instead around the perimeter, the sight of it made Cami's stomach sink. She'd heard about what went on in this place. It was one of the world's best kept secrets ... unless a person's pockets were deep enough.

She'd drained a huge portion of her trust fund to get here. She couldn't afford to screw this up.

Then the trees closed in around their path, blocking the casino from sight. They passed several branches in the walkway before the woman guided her down one. "Those all lead to private villas. I wouldn't suggest you wander down them. While we do provide limited security on the island, if you're too stupid to live, you'll get what's coming to you despite our best efforts."

Cami shook her head. "I'll keep that in mind."

The blonde pulled a key out—Cami had no idea where she'd kept it—and unlocked the front door. "We'll go over all the rules tonight, but the only thing you need to know now is that you can't touch any of the other players until the game begins. If you do, you're immediately disqualified and Death will be displeased. Any rule-breakers will be punished." She gave a mock shudder, though her eyes lit up at the idea of punishment.

"Good to know." Cami stepped into the entryway and turned back. "My luggage?"

"Already delivered. You'll find it in the main bedroom. Last door on the left."

Cami hesitated. "I didn't catch your name."

"I didn't offer it." Another of those sunny grins. "I'm War."

War.

Everyone knew the foursome who ruled the Island of Ys had taken the names of the four horsemen of the apocalypse. No one seemed to know *why*.

Really, the why mattered less than the reputation they'd created. Fierce and brutal and downright vicious to anyone who stood in their way. Cami hadn't been able to find any information on what their ultimate aim was, but it could be as simple and complicated as building power. Either way, they'd created the Island of Ys and built it up to a place where the wealthiest and most powerful people in the world flocked to. They were said to be capable of things that should have been impossible.

She counted on it.

Cami managed to hold out her hand. "It's a pleasure to meet you."

"You're such a liar, little princess." War gave her hand a solid shake and stepped back. "Someone will come for you tonight to escort you to the party. Be ready." She turned and strode away.

Cami stared after her, taking in the tights that had words written up the seam in the back. *Fuck off.* Over and over and over again, in pretty cursive. Cami shook her head and shut the door. If that was one fourth of the group who ruled this island, she wasn't sure what to think of the other three. Or other two, since she'd already interacted with Death. That woman scared her. She'd have to be an idiot *not* to be scared of Death.

The other two, though? Pestilence and Famine?

She didn't know much about Pestilence, other than that he existed. Famine had a long history with Thalania, even if he wasn't inclined to admit it. It wasn't her problem, though. She'd use the connection if she had to, but she wasn't here for him.

She was here for herself and herself alone.

She'd meet them soon enough, it seemed. Cami flipped the lock on the door and moved deeper into the villa. She couldn't afford to assume she had anything resembling privacy while on the island. This place promised to deal in fantasy but that couldn't be where it ended. Why bother to fulfill someone's darkest fantasy if you didn't mean to use it against them later on?

Then again, would people really keep coming back if they thought they were in danger of being outed?

Cami didn't know and, frankly, didn't care. She wasn't here to play out some fantasy, twisted or otherwise. She was here because, for the first time since the Wild Hunt started, Death was offering a special kind of prize to the winner.

A favor.

No caveats. No holds barred. No limits.

Rationally, she was only a woman, if a powerful one. But Cami had spent years researching the Horsemen, following in the footsteps of her mentor who'd devoted even more time and energy into finding out everything there was to know about them. If it was even reasonably possible, Death's favor would cover it. The Horsemen held more power than some countries, hers included.

I want to be free in a way that doesn't hurt the people I love. I want to be able to breathe again, to move freely, to not have the title Princess of Thalania and all its responsibilities dragging me down into the deep.

She meandered through the villa, taking in the second bedroom, the kitchen, the living area, before finally reaching her destination. The master bedroom was wonderful. It was shaped like an octagon, its vaulted ceiling like something out of a dream. Sheer white fabric swung down from a hook in the center of the vault, attaching at two spots over the top of the bed, giving the feeling of a canopy. The doorway opened into a tiled bathroom, complete with walk-in shower and massive tub.

Paradise.

As long as no one looked too closely beneath the surface.

Cami pulled her suitcases onto the bed. Someone would have already gone through them to ensure she hadn't broken the rules—no weapons on the island. She started unpacking slowly, letting the rhythm of the familiar motion soothe her nerves. Five years working toward this goal, and here she was. The hardest part was yet to come, but she couldn't shake the strange feeling like she should be doing more. Her body was so used to running that when she finally stopped, her legs kept trying to move on without her.

So much depended on her ability to succeed in this. She'd broken every rule about putting all her eggs in one basket. This was Cami's one shot. Her only shot. If she failed … Her future stretched out before her in one unbroken line. Marriage to a perfectly pedigreed noble to secure Thalania's internal power base. Children whose only purpose would be to marry more nobles. To look pretty, to pick a charity to support, to dance to the tune set by others. She closed her eyes and took several long breaths.

There was a time, right after her oldest brother returned from exile when she was sixteen, that she'd really believed she could be happy in the palace. Theo had found his happiness, albeit in an unconventional way. If he could do it, then she could, too.

Except one year slid into another and another and another. She hit eighteen and suddenly the responsibilities threatened to choke her, the cage they created tightening every time she took a breath. She'd woken up one morning and the truth crashed over her: the only reason Theo found his happiness was through a full break from Thalania and his being heir to the throne. If he hadn't been exiled, he never would have found Meg, and he and Galen never would have tried to carve out a triad that defied tradition.

As long as she walked along the path laid out for her, she'd never find her true purpose, her true happiness.

She needed that full break that her brother had managed, though Cami didn't see it as a punishment. She just wanted to fly free. Her brother would never forgive her for doing this, for breaking rank and effectively going over his head.

She'd deal with the fallout after she had secured Death's favor. Only then.

"I FUCKING HATE THE WILD HUNT." Luca stood in the shadowed alcove and watched people filter into the room designed for tonight's entertainment. Each contender was allowed three supporting staff to stay on the island, and they'd all brought the full amount. The men wore tuxes. The few women with them wore ball gowns in monochromatic colors, trending toward black.

"This year is important." Ryu, his brother in everything but blood, passed over a bottle of beer. "All the work is paying off. One of *his* people will win, which means he'll be here."

Him. The Bookkeeper.

The first stage of their plan.

There were moments when Luca wished the sins of the past would stay dead and buried, that they could move on with their lives, their success, their power, without digging up this particular evil to exorcise.

He knew better.

The only reason he survived the hell he'd landed in after his abduction was because of Amarante, Ryu, and Kenzie. They were only a couple years older than he was, still children themselves, but they'd protected him as best they were able. They taught him what he had to do in order to keep living day after day, until the moment when freedom was theirs.

He still woke up in a cold sweat more nights than he wanted to admit, the memories of that place riding him hard. It wouldn't end. Fifteen years later, and Luca knew how those kinds of people operated. *His* hell might have been shut down, abandoned, left for the authorities to find, but there were others.

There were always others.

If they didn't cut the head off the snake, once and for all, it would never end. He might not deserve peace, not after what he'd done to survive, but he could help ensure no other children were taken, abused, and discarded like trash when their usefulness had reached its end.

"Luca?"

He gave himself a shake and focused on Ryu. He and Amarante were the only two of the Horsemen related by blood, and like Luca, they actually knew where they came from. For Luca, that was Thalania. For Ryu and Amarante, it was Hong Kong.

His brother looked at him like he wasn't sure if Luca would come apart at the seams. Luca glared. "I'm good. I've got this."

"You sure?" Ryu raked a hand through his short black hair. "Sometimes I wonder if any of us do."

"We have it under control." *Amarante* had it under control. The rest of them would fall in line just like they always did.

Luca turned his attention back to the door. They had dossiers on all the major players participating in this year's Wild Hunt. The mob guy from Boston. The oil heir from Houston. The assassin who was a legend in and of herself. The Bookkeeper's representatives who filled the rest of the slots.

He counted them off as he scanned the room. "Everyone's here."

"Actually ..." Ryu trailed off as *she* walked in. "There's one more."

The white woman wore the palest pink gown, looking like a spring flower that had blossomed in a winter forest. Her cropped dark hair was styled back from her innocent face and she hesitated in the doorway as if she wasn't sure she was in the right place. She *couldn't* be in the right place. Not a spring flower in a winter forest. No, she was a bunny in the midst of hungry wolves. They'd eat her alive.

Luca took a step forward without intending to, and Ryu caught his arm. "We don't interfere."

"That's bullshit and you know it."

Ryu grimaced. "We don't interfere where they can see us."

Luca looked back at the woman. She'd found her

courage and shifted through the crowd, oblivious to the way the men tracked her movements, their gazes following her long after she'd passed. She gracefully took a champagne flute from one of the passing servers and lifted it to pink, pink lips.

Fuck.

"Who is that?"

Ryu was the one who compiled the dossiers in the first place, his ability to track down information downright uncanny. "A late addition."

The hair on the back of Luca's neck stood up. He forced himself to tear his attention from the woman and face his friend, his brother. "Who. The. Fuck. Is. That?"

Ryu shrugged. "That's Princess Camilla Fitzcharles of Thalania, second in line to the throne. Or sixth, I guess, since both her brothers have procreated at this point."

Static blossomed in his head, a roaring he couldn't mute. Luca spun on his heel, ignoring Ryu's curse, and stalked through the crowd toward the little lamb wandering to the slaughter. People got out of his way, but they didn't move far, too intent on watching this little drama play out.

They could keep waiting.

He plucked the champagne flute from her hand, shoved it at a nearby server, and then planted his palm on the small of her back. Christ, she was so tiny, he could practically bracket her waist with his hands if he wanted to. What the fuck was Amarante thinking to invite this little girl to come play, let alone this year of all years?

Camilla let out a little exhale of surprise, but she didn't resist as he all but shoved her through the room and out the door, careful to keep his body between her and the rest of the guests. That sweet submissiveness died the second the door closed behind them.

She stepped away from him, twisting in a move that was as graceful as it seemed second nature. As if she spent a lot of time avoiding men touching her. Fury rose at the thought, fury he had no right to. "What the fuck are you doing here, little girl?"

She swept her dress away from his feet and somehow managed to look down her nose at him despite his having a good foot on her. *Fucking royals*. They were all the same. The few times in the past that Amarante had allowed Thalania's representatives on the island, he'd chosen to make himself scarce. This was different. She might have the snooty thing going for her, but she was as shiny as a new penny.

And as likely to be tossed away by the men in the room behind them.

"I asked you a question."

"I'm deciding if I feel like answering." She eyed him, obviously trying to place him with the rest of them. Luca knew what he looked like. A bruiser who just happened to fill out a tux. Dark hair a little too long, scruff on his jaw where he hadn't bothered to shave, nothing but shadows in his dark eyes. Dangerous.

Because that's exactly what he was. He made no claims otherwise.

So why wasn't she quivering in fear and wilting beneath his gaze?

"You don't get a choice about answering me."

"Don't I?" Her pointed chin rose another notch, her blue eyes flashing. "I have my invitation, the same as the others." Without looking away, she dipped her hand into her tiny purse and fished out a gold embossed invitation with her name scrawled across the front of it.

Princess Camilla Fitzcharles

Goddamn it. Luca barely bit back a growl. He was going

to kick Amarante's ass for this. "I don't give a fuck about the invitation. You're leaving. Now."

"That line of intimidation may work with other representatives Thalania has sent. It won't work with me." She gave him a carefully constructed smile, false and polite. "I'm staying, and I'm competing."

That's what he was afraid of.

The Wild Hunt might not overtly be a fight to the death, but every year there were fatalities. It was a risk the players accepted when they came here. The greatest reward sometimes meant the greatest risk, and the players were all aware of that. No matter what this woman said, she wasn't. She couldn't possibly be. "You will die."

"I might surprise you." She gave a shrug that meant absolutely nothing at all, brushing his words away as easily as she'd brush away new fallen snow.

Or a gnat.

He had to get her out of here. He didn't give a fuck if Amarante invited her. This woman wasn't ready, and her competitors would pick her off early on. She'd be *lucky* if they only killed her.

The thought sank through Luca like a stone in water. He'd never once reacted this way to the people who came to this island to try for whatever prize Amarante had put together. But there'd also never been a fucking *innocent* thinking she could play with the big boys. "Pack your shit. I'm calling the chopper, and you're leaving."

"No." She took a careful step back. At least she knew enough to recognize him as a threat. "Not until I have what I came for."

Luca had done terrible things in his life, things he'd never put into words. People instinctively moved away from him when they saw him coming, whether they knew his reputation or not. And now this little piece of fluff was staring him down as if he couldn't see the pulse thundering away in the hollow of her throat.

"What did you come for?" he ground out.

"Not what. Who." She gave a sad little smile. "I came for you, Luca."

2

Cami might have laughed at the dumbstruck look on Luca's face in response to her lie if the situation wasn't quite so dire. Because he *was* Luca Nibley. Or at least formerly Nibley. She didn't know what surname he went by now. It didn't matter. His grandmother had spent nearly three decades trying to bring him home, and here he stood, healthy and whole. He had the look of the Nibley family—dark hair, dark eyes, and skin that tanned up beautifully in the summer sun.

Cami just hadn't expected him to be so ... large.

He had an air of disreputableness despite his expensive clothing, and the glare his strong features morphed into only reinforced that opinion. He wasn't pleased to see her, and he had no intention of being shuttled back to Thalania to take his place within the Nibley Family.

Just as well.

I'm not actually here for you.

He reached for her again with those massive hands, and she shifted at the last moment, leaving him clutching at air. "It's rude to manhandle."

"It's rude to manhandle," he repeated under his breath as if her words were the dumbest thing he'd ever heard. "Guess what, little girl? You're signing up for a whole lot worse than a hand around your wrist if you enter the Wild Hunt."

"I'm aware." She couldn't quite quell the thrill of fear his statement brought. The primary goal of the Hunt might be to find and capture the so-called White Stag—someone chosen to flee the hunters—but word was that people took out the competition in whatever way they could manage. The fewer people hunting their quarry, the greater their chance of winning.

She would have to be just as ruthless as the others. *More* ruthless.

Heels clicked on the marble, and if Cami hadn't been watching Luca so closely, she would have missed his low curse. He turned to glare at the woman—at War—approaching. She'd changed outfits as well, now dressed in a red gown that plunged nearly to her belly button and had a slit up one side to her hip. It should have looked too daring, too trashy, but somehow she sold it the same way she'd sold her earlier clothing.

Confidence was a wonderful thing.

She narrowed amber eyes at Luca. "I sincerely hope you're not threatening our guest."

"Don't fuck with me. She shouldn't be here and you know it."

War shrugged. "I don't make the rules, I just break them. She was invited, she's now here. End of story."

They squared off like two dogs about to snap and snarl over a choice bone. Cami couldn't tell if this was an angry argument or something resembling a sibling dispute. She had little experience with either. Both her brothers were significantly older and, beyond that, had their paths set out beneath their feet from birth. She wasn't the heir, wasn't the spare. Was simply the third child, the pampered daughter. Raised in relative safety, sheltered from the harsher aspects of the world, and destined to one day marry someone acceptable.

More like a gilded cage.

A cage winning the Wild Hunt would free her from.

Cami carefully lifted her dress so she wouldn't step on it and turned her back on them. They could keep arguing until they were both blue in the face. She was here. It was too late to stop this from happening now, no matter how little Luca seemed to like the idea.

It wasn't his call to make.

War's laugh rolled down the hallway. "Oh my god, I think I'm in love."

"Shut up."

"Don't be mad at me because you want to get all up under that skirt. Not my problem." With another laugh, War hurried to her side and slipped her arm through Cami's, just like she had earlier that day. The only difference was how her fingers dug into Cami's skin. "Keep walking," War murmured. "Don't look back."

"Why not?" Not that she was inclined to look over her shoulder. She already knew what she'd find—Luca glaring a hole in the back of her head as if her very presence insulted him beyond comprehension.

"Because he's liable to stalk over here, toss you over his shoulder, and take you somewhere sinister." War gave a mock shudder. "I mean, that could be really sexy if you're into that sort of thing." She turned that painfully direct gaze on Cami. "*Are* you into that sort of thing?"

"I—What? Why are you asking?"

"No reason." War smiled and opened the door into the room she'd just been unceremoniously hauled from. "You're blushing like a virgin, princess. It's seriously cute. Do you like girls?"

The heat in her cheeks had to have turned her face crimson by now. Cami wasn't blessed with a complexion that would hide her embarrassment. "I ... maybe?"

War stopped shot, her brows slanting down. "Wait a damn minute. *Are* you a virgin? Holy shit, maybe Luca is right. You really shouldn't be here."

"You're doing it again." A deep voice cut in, and Cami could have thrown herself at the newcomer walking up out of sheer relief. He was a beautiful Asian man who moved with a purpose that made her think military, or some kind of specialized security. He frowned at War just like Luca had, their expressions so similar, it left something resonating in Cami's chest.

This is his family.

Not the Nibleys, who had fought so hard to reclaim what they'd lost.

It doesn't matter. Eyes on the prize, Cami.

War gave a put-upon sigh. "Pestilence, this is my good friend Cami. Cami, Pestilence."

He raised his brows at Cami, looking like he was passing some kind of judgement the same way everyone else she'd met since arriving on the island had. Unlike the others, Cami wasn't sure what conclusion he'd come to. "Things are getting started. You're going to want to be closer to the front so you can see."

"Excuse me, we were having a conversation."

Pestilence shook his head and pointed at War. "You have bigger shit to worry about."

Her gaze flicked over Cami's shoulder and something almost serious slipped into her expression. "I guess I do."

Even knowing what to expect, coming to this island was like arriving on a foreign planet. The rules weren't the same, no one acted quite how they should, and danger lurked around every corner. Cami followed them into the room and found an Asian woman presiding over the area. She stood on the small dais that Cami hadn't noticed before, and instead of a gown, she had on a three-piece suit that almost looked like menswear, but significantly more fashionable.

Silence rolled through the room in a wave as people noticed her standing there. The fear and respect that flickered over people's faces in turn told Cami all she needed to know.

She stood in the presence of Death.

Death looked at each of them in turn, her gaze briefly settling on Cami, before moving on. "Welcome to the Island of Ys. You've all been shown to your respective rooms. The Wild Hunt begins in three days." Her voice was low and measured, but a melodious undertone snuck through. It intrigued Cami despite herself. This woman was beautiful the way all the Horsemen seemed to be beautiful, albeit in different ways. The suit showed off her small frame and her black hair was a glossy wave down that fell to halfway down her back. The only color she presented were lips painted a devastating red.

A warning, there.

Cami intended to heed it.

"The prize this year has brought out a new crop of competitors. A White Stag will be named the night before the Hunt begins. The objective is simple. Capture the White Stag. Win the game."

Simple. The very idea was laughable. The Stag would

get nearly twelve hours' head start, and the island where the game came into play had to be at least ten miles long and another few miles wide. Not *that* huge of an area to search … unless one considered the fact it was essentially a jungle, and there would be traps and poisonous creatures and *other* competitors.

You trained for this.

You're as ready as you could possibly be.

That's what she was afraid of. That no matter how ready she was, it wouldn't be enough. She couldn't afford to think like that. Doubt killed just as easily as a gun.

Death spread her arms. "Enjoy our hospitality for now. You will sign your name in three days, and the game will begin." She turned and stepped down from the dais, disappearing through a door Cami hadn't noticed before now, leaving murmurs in her wake.

It was second nature for Cami to pick her way to a nearby alcove and lean against the wall. How many parties had she spent in this exact same position? Watching, never participating. Her oldest brother, the King of Thalania, liked to entertain and the older she got, the more people seemed to expect things of her. Not her brother. Never him. He would never ask her for anything, would never include her in any important decision-making. She was just shy of ten years younger than Theo, and that contributed to his never quite taking her seriously, to always wanting to keep her safe and protected and packed away from anything resembling danger. To him, she would always be a child in need of protection.

This gathering was no different than the ones back in the palace. Oh, the hostilities rode closer to the surface, the smiles knife-sharp, the honeyed words liberally dosed with poison.

A trio of men and a single woman obviously knew each other, and though their features were radically different, they seemed to have pulled their suits from the same rack. They spoke in low voices, and she didn't miss the way they watched the two Horsemen in the room. As if they'd like to end them here and now.

As if they wanted to see them hurt.

Why did the Horsemen allow them here? They're obviously enemies.

She gave an internal shrug and moved on to the next competitor. A large man with dark hair and wary eyes watched the room the same way she did, although he hadn't retreated first. He was the only competitor who hadn't brought anyone with him. He wore his tux with the ease of someone who dressed to the nines often, someone who had been born to money.

Like me.

It would be nice to discount him completely, but there was an air of something akin to desperation in those dark eyes, and it left her cold. She'd avoid this man if she had any choice in the matter. He'd plow through anything that got in his way and to hell with the consequences.

The final man was leaner, but also large, also dark haired and dark eyed. Did they pick these guys out of a mold? His tux was new, and he wore it with ill grace, as if he'd be more comfortable in different clothing. The only people he'd brought were a couple at his back. The woman was small and wore a dress that would be scandalous in higher society. It was a masterpiece of beads and sheer fabric, leaving large swathes of her body exposed to the gaze of everyone in the room. The man at her side exuded such cold menace, no one had dared look at her twice. He also hadn't stopped touching her since they walked through the door, his hand brushing the small of her back, her arm, once even the underside of her breast. Their rings pronounced them man and wife, but Cami didn't need that outward confirmation to know they'd claimed each other. It was there for anyone who cared to look.

The last competitor was a Hispanic woman who wore a slate gray gown that looked to be the height of couture. She chatted easily with the black woman next to her in a paler gray dress. They spoke softly, and though they were easily the most feminine and delicate of the people in this room, they looked at the others like they were prey.

Alarm bells pealed through Cami's head.

I am out of my league.

It didn't matter. It *couldn't* matter.

She smoothed her hands down her gown, feeling very silly and childish in her pastels when everyone else looked like they'd dressed for a different kind of hunt. It would be okay. If they thought she was soft and innocent, they would underestimate her, and that would give her a desperately needed edge.

Cami snagged another glass of champagne and sipped carefully as she kept an eye on the gathering. The only competitors who spoke to each other were the four gathered on the other side of the room. The four on this side, including her, stood apart. Would it be smart to attempt an alliance?

No. Too risky.

If this was a different kind of game, then it might work. Not with the Wild Hunt. They would betray each other at the first opportunity.

"You're outmatched, little girl." His voice curled out of the darkness behind her, low and sinful and downright dangerous.

It took everything in her not to flinch, not to turn so she wasn't presenting him with her back. She'd been *sure* when she took up this position that there was no door behind her. She should have known that this place offered more secrets than readily apparent.

She took another slow sip of her champagne to buy time. "That remains to be seen."

Though he made no sound, he was closer the next time he spoke. She swore she could feel the heat radiating from his large body. "Coming here was a mistake. You might not see it now, but you will before the end of this."

Show no fear.

"I don't make a habit of pursuing mistakes so pointedly. I'm here because I need to be." She kept her posture relaxed through sheer force of will. Cami had never been so thankful for growing up in court as she was in that moment. She'd been taught to create an impenetrable polite mask to keep her thoughts from her face, to eliminate the minute tells of her body that could be translated by anyone who cared to look.

He spoke directly in her ear. "Every time we have this hunt, my sister is named the White Stag. She can't be caught unless she wants to be."

At that, Cami finally turned to face him. He was *much* closer than she'd expected, but she refused to step back even though they were chest to chest. Or, rather, her face to his chest. She resented him forcing her to crane her neck to see his face, resented him even more when she found his expression bathed in shadow.

She lifted her chin. "Then I suppose you have nothing to worry about, do you?" Anger made her rash, made her words into blades. "If there has never been a winner, then I couldn't possibly secure the favor that would bring you home." *Liar, liar, Cami. You have no intention of wasting your favor on that.*

She didn't care. He pissed her off, and she couldn't resist the urge to put him back on his heels.

"That's what none of you Thalanians seem to understand." He made a sound perilously close to a growl. "I *am* home. You're the one who's wandered into a wolf's den, expecting to walk out with every part of you intact." Luca reached up with one of those massive hands and drew a blunt finger over her bottom lip. "If you're lucky, you'll only lose a piece you can go on living without."

Cami's anger dried up. She couldn't think. Couldn't pull away. Could barely move her lips against his finger as her question slipped free. "And if I'm not?"

He dragged that finger down her chin and pressed it unerringly against her heart. "You'll crawl out of here a broken woman. If you crawl out at all."

Her heart kicked against his touch, a warning and something altogether less acceptable. Cami took a slow step back, and Luca let his hand fall back to his side. She shook her head. "You won't scare me away from this. I wish you'd stop trying."

"They always did breed you royals with more good looks than sense. Do you have any idea how fucking breakable you are?"

If he only knew.

A quiver worked its way through her, and she didn't quite have enough mastery over herself to stem it. He saw. Of course he saw. He followed her into the light, a slow stalk that had her tensing, her body clamoring to run or fight because she was definitely in danger and the source of it towered over her, seeming to block out every ray of light in the room. "Give me some room," she bit out.

"Plenty of room in this world. All you need to do is get your tight little ass back on the chopper and leave the island. Simple enough that even a sheltered little girl like you can figure it out."

He wanted to scare her, to infuriate her.

To her shame, it worked.

It would be the easiest thing in the world to do what he wanted. To allow herself to be shuttled back to her plane, to return to the comforting embrace of her country and the palace. To settle back into the cage she'd spent her entire life trapped in. To be Princess Camilla, a woman who never stepped out of line or did anything surprising.

If she did that, the flame she'd spent five years so carefully nurturing would be snuffed out for good. No more freedom. No more adventure. Nothing but the expected from now until the moment she died, likely of old age after being shuttled away to some comfortable country estate.

No. Absolutely not.

She *refused*.

She'd worked too hard to get to this moment, and she'd be damned before she let this big brute intimidate her. Cami reclaimed the step she'd taken in retreat, bringing them nearly chest to chest again. "Maybe you find it so easy to shirk from your promises, Luca Nibley, but I take mine seriously."

He still looked like he might do exactly what War had threatened and toss Cami over his shoulder, so she went in for the kill, the one thing guaranteed to get him off her back. "Or did you forget that I'm your fiancée? We've been promised to each other since we were children."

3

Luca stared down at Camilla, her words ringing through his mind. *We've been promised to each other since we were children.* He hadn't remembered. Why should he? The years he'd spent in his childhood home, before he was stolen away and shoved into hell, were like something out of a dream. As substantial as mist.

If she spoke the truth, this was a foolish promise that went back something like twenty-five years. No one in their right mind would expect him to honor it.

Except she stood here, her blue eyes challenging him to do exactly that.

"You're out of your goddamn mind."

"Am I?" She shrugged a single shoulder. "Then I suppose you had better leave me to it."

He wanted to shake her, to kiss that pretty pink mouth until all her carefully constructed poise disappeared to reveal the wild thing underneath. Luca gave himself a shake. What was he thinking? There was no wild thing inside this woman. If he shattered her exterior, he would break her. There was nothing of substance beneath.

He glanced over her head to the rest of the room. They had everyone's attention now. He clenched his jaw. "It won't work. I'm not coming back to play the spoiled nobleman or the devoted husband or whatever other fantasy you've constructed."

She stared at him for several long moments. "You'd force Death to break her word?"

Yeah, he was definitely going to kick Amarante's ass for this. She had always played the deeper game, and he'd been content to let her do it. Luca owed her that, at the very least. But even his bone-deep gratitude only went so far. They were supposed to be partners, the four of them, and that agreement didn't include her inviting innocents into their plans.

Especially when the innocent in question was under the mistaken belief that she was betrothed to Luca.

"We are not engaged," he spoke slowly, drawing each word out as if speaking to a child. "Consider yourself lucky. You've dodged a bullet."

"That remains to be seen." She turned without another word and strode away, the very picture of a tiny queen moving through the room as if she had every right to be there.

He had to concentrate on standing still and not following her. He clenched his fists, watching her until she disappeared through the door. There was absolutely nothing stopping someone from hurting her. This island might be all carefully constructed fantasy, but real risk occasionally slipped through. The responsible party was always punished, was *always* made an example of.

But it still happened despite their best efforts.

His eyes found Ryu casually leaning against the wall, speaking softly with Kenzie. Ryu raised a single brow at whatever look Luca had written across his face, but he pushed away from the wall and followed Camilla through the door.

Luca melted back into the shadows of the alcove. There was a door hidden in the panels near the corner, but he merely waited. Watching.

Slowly, oh so slowly, conversation started up again. The Texan heir left first, stalking through the door as if he couldn't stand to remain in the room a second longer. Then the mob guy, trailing his sponsors behind him. The assassins, both as pretty as a picture, showed no signs of leaving, seeming to enjoy the free food and whatever they were discussing. Only one of them would be competing, but that didn't make the other any less dangerous.

An invitation had been secured, but the final list of competitors would be finalized the night before the hunt. That's when Amarante would announce that Kenzie was the White Stag, and Kenzie would leave for the larger island. Twelve hours were more than enough for her to ensure her win. All four of them knew every secret that island had to offer, from the cameras situated to give spectators the best views of the action to the carefully concealed traps meant to trip up the unwary. They made millions each year on the betting alone, people with more money than sense loved to pick favorites and cheer them on.

He hadn't been lying. Kenzie had never been caught. She might not look it to an outsider, but if she ever wanted to, she could meld into the woods anywhere in the world and never be seen again.

A skill that had kept them alive when they needed it most.

He gave himself another shake. The past lingered at the edges of his mind, flickering like some dark flame intent on consuming his thoughts. He couldn't afford to be distracted now. They had things to accomplish, a plan two decades in the making that was finally, *finally*, being put into motion.

Luca made himself turn from the room and push the ridged spot on the wall that opened the door. He slipped through, paused to ensure it was securely closed behind him, and then moved through the dark passageways that crisscrossed both casinos on the small island. Some of them were used by staff, but others were known only to him and his siblings. The benefit of the ability to move without being seen was priceless at times.

Like now.

He made his way to the hub, the spot where they ran all the operations on the island, and the place where they each kept their private rooms. As expected, he found Amarante standing before the wall of monitors, her gaze on the room he'd just vacated.

She hadn't changed out of the suit, but she'd pulled her long black hair away from her face. Without looking at him, she said, "You're distracted."

"No shit." He stopped next to her. Even though he knew better, he still tracked the cameras leading to the competitors' villas. Camilla moved through one, her pace steady, her expression perfectly calm. As if nothing could touch her. She didn't seem to notice Ryu shadowing her steps, and that should please him. If she thought for a second that he cared whether she lived or died, she'd take it as a sign that she had a chance in hell of prying Luca out of this place. She didn't.

But that didn't mean he wanted her harmed.

Getting soft.

"Do you remember the plan?"

He dragged his gaze from the monitors to find Amarante watching him closely. Of course he remembered. Of the four of them, Luca had spent the least amount of time in that hell. It was Amarante who approached him after he won that first fight, when he was just a terrified ten-year-old who only wanted to go home, and taught him how to survive that place.

It was Amarante who'd pushed them to keep going, to keep fighting, when they traveled by foot south to Seattle, a group of motley kids who shouldn't have survived.

And it was Amarante who'd crafted this plan to ensure what happened to them would never happen to anyone else again.

"It's really shitty of you to remind me of that every time you think I'm going to break ranks. I'm here, Amarante. This is my home. You are my people. Of course I fucking remember the plan. I want them ground to dust, the same as you." He had to fight the urge to look at the monitors again. "But if you wanted me not to be distracted, why the hell did you invite her to play this game? We don't fuck with innocents."

"Innocents," she said the word like she was tasting it. "She's not a child. She made her choice. Who am I to hold her back?"

As much as he loved Amarante, he spent a good portion of their time together wanting to throttle her. She never came at a goal directly, preferring to skirt the edges, nudging all the players into place before she began the games.

She'd just never played those games with *them*.

"What are you up to?"

"They came." She nodded at the monitor showing the room. "I told you they would."

He gave an inward sigh. Apparently the topic of Camilla was closed. Luca studied the three men and single woman who were all sponsored by the Bookkeeper. The man in question—at least, they were reasonably sure it was a man behind the money—lost a small fortune to them over the years, especially around the Wild Hunt. Money he'd earned by trafficking children, among other things.

This year, a carefully crafted invitation had gone out directly to him. A taunt, though it wasn't overtly categorized as such. As a result, he'd weighed the competition in his favor by sponsoring four competitors. Technically, he was only allowed one, and his shell corporations sponsored the other three, but Ryu had tracked the money back to the source.

They had him on the line.

"Once we do this, there's no going back," Luca finally said.

"Second thoughts?"

"No." He'd given up wondering what his life would have been like if he wasn't stolen away from his safe little family in Thalania. That kind of hope could kill a person in the place he'd met Amarante—a lesson she'd taught him herself. There was no before. There was only now.

They survived.

More than that, they'd used the skills they learned, the fury, the complete and utter ruthlessness, to carve out a piece of the world that was theirs and theirs alone. No one could touch them on the little trio of islands they owned off the coast of Africa. It was their world, their rules, their game board.

"You're sure he'll come." He didn't quite phrase is as a question, but she answered all the same.

"He'll have to once he wins. He won't be able to resist taunting us when he collects his favor."

A risk, and a large one at that. Some sponsors liked to hide in the shadows, allowing their competitors to act in proxy. There was always the possibility that someone would go rogue, though, and that's what they banked on in this scenario. The Bookkeeper wanted the prize too much to risk it.

Which meant he had to think he could win in order to tempt him to the island.

"Is Kenzie up to this?"

Amarante gave him the look that question deserved. "It's covered."

Was it? Because the one thing Kenzie couldn't stand was being trapped. She played parts like she thought life was nothing but a stage, but the second she was cornered, she went for someone's throat. In all the time he'd known her, she'd never been able to master that knee-jerk reaction. "If she kills the winner—"

"It's covered, Luca." Amarante gave him a tight smile. "Trust me."

With his life? Always. She'd earned that trust and more. Amarante would never do something to directly harm him or the others. *That*, he believed beyond a shadow of a doubt.

Everyone else was fair game, though.

Including little Camilla Fitzcharles.

CAMI KNEW someone was following her, but they didn't shadow her steps as she turned toward her villa, so she didn't bother worrying about it. There was already too much occupying her mental space as it was. Obviously the person behind her hadn't meant her harm, and that was all she needed to know.

Especially when she had so many other things to worry about.

No one had won the Wild Hunt before.

Cami slipped into her villa and locked the door behind her. She moved through the space without turning on any lights, checking to ensure she was still alone. Cameras remained a potential issue, but she ignored that problem the same way she'd ignored the person following her to her villa.

Satisfied she was alone, she stripped out of her gown and hung it up in the closet. The air conditioner hummed softly, fighting a valiant battle against the clammy heat hovering on the other side of these walls. The humidity was cloying, wrapping around her the second she walked out the door. If she hadn't already cut off most of her hair, she would have considered taking it to the chopping block just to keep it off her face and neck.

She pulled on her short silk robe and considered her options. Three more days until the hunt began. She hadn't wanted that time when she first arrived here, had desired only to jump straight into the competition and finish what had been started so long ago.

Her bid for freedom.

She laughed softly. The look on Luca's face when she told him they were engaged. He honestly thought she'd come all this way, was about to engage in a deadly game because she wanted to be married to him that badly. Cami laughed again. Men were strange creatures, but he'd laid the foundation for her lie when he flipped out the second he saw her.

Guilt flared, hot and cloying. She *should* be here to bring him home. That's what a good girl would do in this situation. Cleave to the family honor that demanded she follow through on the promise her older brother hadn't been able to accomplish in the years since he'd retaken the throne.

Retrieve Luca safely.

An impossible feat when he didn't *want* to be retrieved.

She'd spent the last five summers working directly under Lady Nibley. She'd heard the story of his disappearance enough times to have it memorized, right down to the tears that sprung into the old woman's eyes at the thought of never seeing her beloved grandson again before she died. Yael had been fighting to bring Luca home since the day he disappeared, and the failure to do so weighed on her.

Even with that knowledge sitting heavy in her chest, Cami couldn't ignore the fact that Luca was free here in a way he'd never be back in Thalania. Free in the way Cami wanted to be free. Here, he was one of the four people who could do anything they wanted, who had more money that most countries and the influence to match.

She envied him that.

A ringing brought her back to herself. Her phone. She sighed. It could only be one of three people on the other line—her brother or one of his two Consorts. None of them would have kind words for her, but if she didn't answer, it would be so much worse.

If I want to be taken seriously, dodging their calls isn't the way to do it.

Neither is running off to play a real-life version of The Most Dangerous Game, either. Probably.

She'd happily avoid answering, but if she put off her brother, he was more than capable of sending a battalion to retrieve her. Or, worse, sending his head of security and Consort—Galen.

Cami pulled her phone out and cleared her throat. *Calm and collected.* "Hello?"

"Where the fuck are you?"

Apparently she was the only one interested in being

calm and collected. "I left a note. It was a very detailed and concise note."

She couldn't be sure, but she thought she could hear Theo grinding his teeth even from here. "The note states, 'I've gone to the Island of Ys.' That's the sum of it. That is hardly detailed *or* concise."

"I beg to differ."

"He's not coming home, Cami. You think I haven't spent six years trying? Lady Nibley might not believe it, but I expect *you* to. Luca wants to stay gone. And unlike some, I'm not willing to attempt kidnapping." Theo sighed. "Come home. Whatever you're trying to do ... There's a better way. You know damn well I wouldn't push you into marrying *anyone* you didn't want, let alone some half-feral stranger. You care for Lady Nibley, and that's understandable, but—"

"I'm not coming home." She spoke slowly, clearly, not letting anything into her voice but confidence. Certainly not the hurt that her brother thought all she cared about was honoring some ancient promise to marry her to a stranger. Did he really think that was all she cared about?

Did *everyone* think that was all she cared about?

Yes, she wanted to convince Luca to come home long enough to see his grandmother before she died, but Cami had bigger game in mind than securing herself a husband. She was twenty-three. She wasn't interested in marrying *anyone* for a very long time. And she certainly wasn't going to hunt down some angry man whom she'd have to hogtie to get to the altar.

Though the image of Luca hogtied was an attractive one, he'd probably still try to command her obedience. He seemed like the kind of man who couldn't comprehend people not doing everything he ordered the second he ordered it. He'd been almost flabbergasted when she ignored his threats. She might have laughed if the stakes were anything less than life and death.

Her life.

Her freedom.

Her everything.

"Cami." Another sigh, world-weary this time. "I know you're not happy with me right now, but this isn't the way to go about it."

Not happy with him.

Cami sank onto the bed. Trust Theo not to circle the subject when he could strike right to the heart of her. "You called me home early from Yael's country home like a dog. Or a disobedient child. You sent Isaac *and* Galen to collect me. My very own prison guards."

"The palace is not a prison."

"Says you." Anger bled into her voice, and she had to take several moments to reclaim her control. "You agreed to give me the summers, and then you went back on it the first time something came up." Her summers were the only time of year she felt both happy and free. Happy soaking up all Yael's not-inconsiderable knowledge. Everyone in Thalania treated the old woman with respect and no little amount of fear. Cami didn't want people to fear her, but she wanted the freedom power brought. Freedom Lady Nibley enjoyed.

But it was different for a Head of Family than it was for a princess.

Something she learned the hard way a few short weeks ago.

Another of those sighs. "I needed you back at the palace." For her brother, it was as simple as that. He needed her there, so it didn't matter what she wanted. "I—correctly —assumed I'd have to use a crowbar to pry you out of her country estate."

A crowbar in the form of his husband and Consort, one third of the Royal Triad.

"To dangle me in front of that Saudi mogul like some kind of prize." If not for Theo pulling rank, she might have put off the Wild Hunt for years yet. But the betrayal cut too deep. He'd promised her a chance to choose a husband for herself. He'd promised her *time*.

"You treated me like a pawn to move around at whim," she whispered. That moment of being brought back to the palace like an errant child had slammed her with one undeniable truth.

As long as she was Camilla Fitzcharles, Princess of Thalania, she'd never have a chance to be anything else.

Cami just wanted to be free. Free to choose her own path. Free of the strings threatening to bind her up like a tangled marionette.

"Come home, Cami. That's an order."

Just like that, her sadness evaporated in a fury that left her breathless. "Goodbye, Theo." She hung up and turned her phone off. He might try to send someone for her. Let him come. Somehow, she didn't think Death would take too kindly to having Thalanian royals screwing around on her territory. Cami had her invitation. There was no going back now.

She pulled the card out of her purse and set it on the pale wood dresser. Letting Luca think she was here to secure him as a husband was more than a little mean, but if he thought she was an empty-headed idiot, he would underestimate her. The others would follow his lead, she was sure of it.

No one would know what she was capable of until she'd secured the first win in the Wild Hunt history.

Cami had to believe it would spin out that way. To do

anything else would be the equivalent of shooting herself in the foot before a marathon. She'd prepared. She'd trained. She'd done everything in her power to stack the deck in her favor.

Only time would tell if it was enough.

4

After the party Luca spent two days in Pain dealing with a politician who had tried to rough up one of their people. While sex was one of the things peddled on the island, it was heavily regulated. Every once in a while, they had issues with people thinking that *every* employee was fair game.

He'd had to make an example of the man, and then he'd needed to stay to ensure the girl was okay. The assault was stopped almost as quickly as it had started, but it scared the shit out of her. Understandable, that. He'd given her two weeks' extra pay and arranged to have her moved to Pleasure until she felt comfortable in Pain again—if she ever did. Ultimately, he left the choice up to her.

He'd almost convinced himself to let this shit with Camilla go. If she wanted to play with the big boys, she'd get smacked down—even hurt—but he couldn't let it be his problem. He had to keep his focus on the endgame.

Fifteen years, they'd looked for the people responsible and came up with nothing. Their tormentors all wore masks while they were in hell, and no record of that place existed.

If there had been, Ryu would have found it by now. The only lead they could scrounge up was with the Bookkeeper, which meant that fucker was the key to everything.

The key to every operation, both aboveboard and dirty, lay in its money. One look at their enemy's books and they could find the exact pressure point they needed to find out who the bastards responsible were and to bring them to their knees.

To remove them once and for all.

This game had to play out exactly as Amarante planned. For better or worse. He didn't know why she'd brought Camilla here and, frankly, he didn't care. The princess was secondary to everything else.

He still didn't expect Ryu's call. Luca stared at his phone a long time and finally answered. "Yeah?"

"We need you back here for the dinner tonight. Amarante wants to present a united front."

Of course she did. Luca didn't exactly resent her for what she'd put together, but there were times when he wished they could all leave the goddamn past where it lay. Dredging up all those old nightmares—nightmares that had never fully gone away in the first place—meant all four of them would be careening close to the edge until this was over. Their semblance of normal would fall apart, and he didn't know where they'd land. In the past, they'd always leaned on each other when shit got too dark to see their way through.

Then that's what we'll do in the future.

We've started this, tipped the first domino.

It's time to finish it.

Maybe then he could finally get a little slice of that peace he kept hearing about, and the ragged wounds in his chest would finally heal into something smooth and forgiving.

Maybe.

He huffed out a breath. "She go home?"

Ryu didn't bother to ask who he meant. "You know she didn't."

Yeah, he guessed he did. The princess wasn't leaving unless someone forced the issue. It wasn't his call to make, but her presence represented a dangerous distraction that none of them could afford. "I'll be at dinner."

"Six."

He glanced at his watch. Plenty of time to make the walk back to Pleasure and change. After two days being cooped up inside, he was ready to stretch his legs some. "See you then." He hung up and headed for the exit.

When they'd first bought this place, the only thing on this island was an old rotted resort that had gone up sometime in the sixties and promptly failed. They built it back up from the bottom, and turned it into the place it was now. Part paradise, part fantasy island, part something significantly darker. Though there were days when Luca wished they'd let the jungle take this island back the same way they'd let it take the larger island back, that they'd merely carved out a small part of it for them and them alone, he couldn't quite hate the island itself.

He started down the boardwalk that stretched across the length of the bay, connecting Pleasure and Pain if someone was feeling ambitious enough to walk the distance. Little shops crowded one side of the boardwalk, offering everything from gourmet food to entertainment to cool courtyards to rest in. On the other side lay the beach, the white sand stretching to disappear beneath bright blue water.

It was hot and sticky, and if guests wanted to swim this time of year, they gravitated to pools in both casinos or rented the private villas on the western edge of this island.

Sometimes a stray person or two would drunkenly wander into this bay and have to be fished out, but for the most part, they kept off the beach.

Luca kicked off his shoes and walked to the point where sand met water. Right here, right now, he could almost ignore the busy boardwalk to his left.

It didn't matter.

They didn't matter. The rich-ass people who came here to get their rocks off. They were only a means to an end, and their selfishness funded a cause greater than their own. It didn't make him hate them less during the dark of the night, but they served their purpose. Same as him.

Luca kept his pace steady and inhaled the salty sea air. It relaxed the thing coiled tightly in his chest. It might be temporary, but it was better than nothing. He picked his way up the beach, keeping an eye on the buzzing people on the boardwalk, but leaving them to it. Most of them were here to watch and bet on the Wild Hunt, and the air practically crackled with their excitement.

If they only knew.

Up ahead, nearly in the shadow of Pleasure, a series of lounge chairs had been set up. They were mostly used by drunken guests who couldn't quite make it back to their rooms from the boardwalk, but today a woman reclined in one.

Luca recognized her even from this distance, and he hated himself a little for having that much familiarity. If he had half a goddamn brain, he'd veer up to the boardwalk and avoid her, but his feet didn't get the memo. Each stride brought him closer to her, details becoming stark in the decreasing distance.

Large sunglasses covering her eyes.

The bikini top that seemed designed to tease, the tiny

triangles leaving the curves of her breasts bare and barely held in place with two feeble strings. An inch each way and he'd see what color her nipples were.

The bottoms were no better. They drew his gaze from her belly button down, down, down to the mound they barely kept hidden. If she rolled over, he had no doubt that her tight little ass wouldn't be covered in the least.

Christ.

He should walk away. He had no business doing anything else. She wasn't his problem, something he'd congratulated himself on not an hour ago.

Where the hell did a protected little princess get a swimsuit like *that?*

And why the fuck had her older brothers let her out of their country with it?

Luca stalked closer, until his shadow fell over her pale body. This close, he caught the faint scent of her coconut tanning lotion, and hell if his mouth didn't start to water. It was all too easy to picture tugging that swimsuit aside and making a mess of her. Of both of them.

He looked away. What the fuck was wrong with him? He didn't do this shit. He wasn't a saint, but he didn't spend time lusting after women who didn't move in his world, weren't right there in the dirt with him. Tarnishing something pure wasn't his kink, and he wasn't about to start now.

Except he couldn't stop himself from looking at her again, from dragging his gaze over her cropped dark hair, down that long pale neck, over her perky breasts, and down to where that triangle of red barely covered her pussy. Would she be bare there? Or left natural?

Get a hold of yourself, asshole.

She draped one arm over her head, her breasts straining dangerously against the swimsuit top. "You're staring."

"You put that suit on. You wanted men to stare."

"Maybe." Her lips curved in something that was almost a smile. "It's still rude."

"Little girl, you're inviting me to do a whole lot more than stare."

She lifted her sunglasses and squinted at him. "Huh."

Huh?

Luca found himself leaning forward, drawn to her in a way he couldn't quite combat. "What's that supposed to mean?"

"I know your life hasn't exactly been easy, but let's squash the rape-y talk, okay? Contrary to popular belief, it's not sexy."

He rocked back on his heels. "What the fuck are you talking about?"

"*Little girl, you're inviting me to do a whole lot more than stare.*" With her voice lowered, she did a passably good impression of him. Camilla raised her eyebrows. "Didn't those words just come out of your mouth?"

Luca had the insane urge to squirm. Like she'd caught him out at something. "Christ." He ran his hand over his face. "You're safe from me, Princess. I only play with women who want it."

Camilla gave him a long look and dropped her sunglasses back into place, shielding those blue, blue eyes from him. "And if I want it?"

His body gave a resounding *fuck yes* before he caught himself. Luca narrowed his eyes. "You're fucking with me."

There went that little smile again. "You come at every conversation with me like a bull in a china shop. All I have to do is wave a red flag and ..." She motioned down at herself, at her bright red suit. "Honestly, it's too easy. Low hanging fruit and all that."

That surprised a chuckle out of him. "I thought princesses were supposed to be proper and polite."

"What gave you that idea?"

He looked at her again, really looked at her. She wasn't uncomfortable or self-conscious in that suit. She wore it like she'd spent a lot of time waltzing around in next to nothing. Luca tilted his head to the side, studying her. "If you think seduction is going to work, you're fucked in the head."

She laughed, the sound light and bell-like. It made her breasts shake, just a little. Just enough to make a man like him wonder how they'd bounce if she was riding his cock. *Damn it.*

Camilla rolled over and fuck if the back of that bikini covered even less than he'd suspected. It was little more than a thong, leaving the round curves of her ass bare. She motioned a leisurely hand at the striped bag next to her chair. "Be a darling and lotion my back, would you?"

Luca should have walked away right then and there. He knew a trap when he saw it, and this entire situation screamed *danger* in a way that had his instincts thrumming. Getting the fuck out of there was the only option.

He dug into the bag and grabbed the suntan lotion.

CAMI HADN'T ACTUALLY THOUGHT he'd do it. For all her teasing about him being a bull in a china shop, *she* was the one waving the red flag in front of his face and then being surprised when he charged her. She tried to relax, tried to act like she couldn't feel his gaze dragging down her nearly-bare back to settle on her ass.

"Lot of real estate here," he murmured as she heard him squirt lotion onto his hand.

Oh my god, he's going to touch me.

She tensed, ready to call the whole thing off, but then his palm was there, spreading warm lotion onto her back. The only warning she got was a slight pull on the strings of her top and then it went loose, falling on either side of her body. *He just untied my top.* She blinked. "Forward of you."

"No point in doing a job unless you do it right." His voice was lower than before, rumbling like the first stirrings of an earthquake. He smoothed his big hand down her spine again and then both hands were there, carefully rubbing the lotion into her skin. His callouses dragged over her skin, sending sparks of pleasure in their wake, and his strength was clear in every movement of his fingers against her tight muscles.

I wasn't prepared.

This was a mistake.

"Relax, Camilla. I'm not going to rip off your swimsuit and fuck you right here in front of god and everyone on the boardwalk."

"Cami." The word escaped on a sound that was almost a whisper.

He paused. "Hmm."

"I prefer Cami."

Luca started up again. He went back for more lotion and spent an inordinate amount of time on her shoulders and arms. Despite everything, she couldn't help relaxing. It felt good. She couldn't remember the last time someone touched her like this ... If they *ever* had. She'd had boyfriends, sure, but if they weren't too terrified of her brothers to pull any moves like this in public, the only time they used a back rub was as a quick prelude to other things.

This ...

This felt like the main event.

Luca stroked his hands down her sides, his fingers unabashedly tracing the sides of her breasts where they were pressed against the lounge chair. She shivered—she couldn't help it—and he cursed softly. "You're nothing but trouble."

"And yet I'm the one just lying here."

He snorted. "Bullshit." Luca reached her hips and paused, his fingers resting lightly on the top edge of her swimsuit. When he spoke again, his voice was lower yet. Thick with desire. "Sun's strong down here by the equator. Would be a shame for you to burn something sensitive."

He's asking permission.

She should say no. Should make her excuses and get the hell out of there. For all that she enjoyed provoking him, he wasn't hers to seduce, and she certainly shouldn't let *him* do the seducing, either.

But there in that moment, she couldn't quite make her lips form the correct words. The heat of the sun had soaked right down to her bones, the soft sound of the waves coming in intoxicated her, and the feeling of Luca's hands on her body was too good to stop. *Not yet. Just a little more.* "It would be a shame, wouldn't it?"

"Mmhmm." He stopped touching her long enough to get more lotion. She half expected him to start straight on her ass, but apparently Luca was intent on surprising her. He shifted back and began at her left ankle, working the lotion into her leg. Up and up he climbed, inch by inch, stopping at the lower curve of her ass.

And then he moved to her right leg.

Cami couldn't breathe. He hadn't touched her in any meaningful place and yet she was so turned on, she couldn't think straight. Her blood pounded through her body, her muscles going soft, a throbbing need pulsing between her thighs. She pressed her forehead hard against the lounge chair, but the pressure was no match for Luca's hands working ever upward on her right leg.

Again, he stopped just as the lower curve of her ass.

He dragged his thumbs on identical paths mirroring the swimsuit bottom. Low on her hips and down to her crease. "Beautiful." She was one hundred percent certain he hadn't meant to say that aloud, but Cami didn't care. He couldn't take it back. He massaged her ass, cupping and squeezing until she panted with need and parted her legs slightly. An invitation she wasn't sure she'd meant to make, but she didn't want to take back.

Another of those delicious low curses that seemed dragged from his lips. "You were sent to torment me."

"Maybe." Though she was the one being tormented. If he didn't touch her soon …

"I wonder." He gripped her upper thighs and nudged them a little farther apart, lifting her ass the tiniest bit. "If I pulled this tease of a suit aside, would I find you wet and aching for me?"

Now was the time to deescalate. To say something to spark his temper so he'd leave her in peace. "Look and find out."

"Wicked little thing, aren't you?" He hooked her suit with his thumb and tugged it to the side. "Christ. I can see your need from here."

She shivered. "Touch me. Please."

"Nah, I don't think so." His hand shook, just a little, where he gripped her ass while he held her suit to the side with the other. She could *feel* his gaze there as if he'd stroked her.

Pleasure coiled tightly through her, almost painful. "Please, Luca. Touch me."

"You're an independent woman, and you've sure as fuck proven you don't take orders from me. You want that orgasm you're craving? To come quick and dirty right here with people up on that boardwalk not knowing the difference?"

"Yes," she practically sobbed the word.

"Then *take* it." He yanked her suit fully to the side, her body jerking with the force of the movement, and then she felt the weight of his hand an inch below her barely spread thighs. "Back up onto my hand. Use me."

She couldn't. It was a step too far. She might want him in this moment, but this was a mistake.

Cami slid back that inch that separated them, gasping when his big hand cupped her bare pussy. "Oh god."

"This doesn't have anything to do with god, and you damn well know it. This is sin, pure and simple." His voice went rough and tight and he lifted his fingers slightly, right against her clit. "Ride my hand. Take what you need."

She shouldn't ...

But the thought had no weight here in this strange moment of in-between. Cami rocked back onto his hand and then forward. The slightest movement that sent a spiral of pleasure through her. She whimpered and did it again. This was so wrong. There were people *right there*.

She couldn't stop.

Not with his low words reaching across the negligible distance between them, seeming to be pulled from him despite his best intentions. "Naughty girl, using me like this. You love that shit, don't you? I could be anyone. Some schmuck who wandered over to help you lotion up, letting you grind on him while he thinks about taking you back to his villa to fuck you seven ways to Sunday."

This wasn't happening because of some random guy, though. This was solely because of Luca, and the lure he exuded that she responded to despite herself. It was *him* touching her so intimately, flexing his fingers ever so slightly every time she rocked against them. Her breathe sobbed out. "It's not enough. Too much. I don't know."

"Don't stop." The command lashed her, and she thrust back against his touch, grinding herself hard against his palm.

There. Yes. She gripped the sides of the lounge chair by her hair and bit her lip hard as she came. "Oh shit." Cami closed her eyes and tried to focus on recovering. On figuring out how to get out of his situation gracefully.

Luca flexed his fingers again.

She moaned. She couldn't help it.

"Greedy girl," he ground out. "You'd keep fucking my hand until the sun goes down, wouldn't you? Grinding that sensitive little clit against my fingers, coming all over my palm." He dragged his hand out from beneath her slowly, stroking her as he did. "Yeah, that's exactly what you'd do. Have to wonder if you'd do the same on my mouth?" A sound, and she knew beyond a shadow of a doubt that he'd just sucked his fingers, wet from her orgasm, into his mouth. "Fuck, Cami, but you're something else."

"Thanks?" Was that her voice? So breathy and, yes, needy.

She wanted more.

The realization had her biting back a whimper. She had no business wanting this man. Wanting *any* man on this island. What had gotten into her?

You know what.

Or, rather, who.

He must have seen her tense up, because he pulled her swimsuit back into place and then tied her top straps again, all business. "Dinner's at six."

By the time she managed to lift her head, he was gone, just a figure striding up the sand to the walkway leading back to the casino. If her body wasn't thrumming with pleasure and satisfaction from her orgasm, Cami almost could have convinced herself it never happened. Or that she didn't desperately wanted it to happen again.

Almost.

5

Cami took her time dressing for dinner. Even though the mirror told her otherwise, she couldn't shake the feeling that her body still maintained the flush of her earlier orgasm. It felt tattooed on her skin, written for anyone who cared to look. She wanted to seek Luca out, to ask him how they'd gone from sniping at each other to *that*, but doing so meant showing her hand. The only protection she had at this point was the aloofness she gathered around herself like a cloak.

She studied her gown. It was high-necked and white, though the back was mostly nonexistent. It flared from her hips and would kick out a little with each step she took, giving the impression she floated an inch above the ground. She had a closet full of dresses at home, but she'd very specifically chose the virginal ones for this trip. The ones designed to make her look young, innocent, and breakable.

An enemy who underestimates you is an enemy you can beat.

Yael's gravelly words rolled through her and she pressed her hand to her chest. She missed that cranky old woman. Five summers spent in the Nibley country house and she felt closer to Lady Nibley than she had to most of her own family.

She couldn't win this without the training and knowledge Yael had imparted during those summers spent together.

Cami took half a second to make sure her pink lipstick was in place and then she left her villa. Prolonging seeing Luca again wouldn't make a single bit of difference in the Hunt, and she couldn't risk being late and ending up disqualified before the games even began.

Fifteen minutes later, she was led to the same room they'd had drinks three nights ago. Cami didn't allow herself to pause in the doorway this time. She drifted into the room, vividly aware of eyes on her. No point in theorizing their impressions. It was clear to anyone who cared to look. Interest on a few of the men's faces. Curiosity on one of the women's.

Two of the four low tables were fully occupied, leaving her with the options of the two women she'd seen the first night, or the dangerous-looking man with his sponsors who she'd overheard someone referencing as mob people. Russian or Irish or both—Cami hadn't been quite clear on that. The fact the women were the only people seated at *their* table, though, told her everything she needed to know.

The mob people were the lesser of two evils.

She walked up to the empty chair and touched the back of it lightly. "Is this seat taken?"

The woman glanced at her with interest. "Not at all. Sit." Her husband made a low sound that might have been a laugh and she glanced at him. "What? The longer she stands there, the more likely she is to change her mind."

Curiosity flared and Cami slid into the empty seat. She extended her hand. "Camilla Fitzcharles."

"Fitzcharles of the Thalanian Fitzcharleses?" The woman took her hand and gave it a solid shake. "Keira. This is my husband, Dmitri." She jerked her thumb at the man on her other side. "This is Liam. Not to be a total dick or anything, but he's going to kick your ass in the Hunt."

Liam sighed. "Keira. Some tact wouldn't be ill advised."

"Do you know how many favors we had to pull to get you into this thing? I don't have to be tactful."

Cami laughed. She couldn't help it. "They certainly don't make it easy, do they?" She offered her hand. "It's nice to meet you, Liam. Even if the friendship won't last the night."

He took Cami's hand. He really was quite attractive, in the tall, dark, and handsome sort of way. Big, though not as big as Luca. Much more polished as well. This man was dangerous, but he didn't beat a person over the head with that fact. He pressed a perfectly polite kiss to her knuckles. "The pleasure's all mine."

She started to say something to keep the small talk going, but the door at the back of the room opened and all four Horsemen walked into the room. Death came first, wearing another suit that spoke of menswear but managed to be so feminine and sexy that it stole Cami's breath. Next was War in another red gown that almost seemed made of liquid, clinging to her body sensuously. Pestilence and Luca moved as one, again reinforcing a familial resemblance that had nothing to do with the surface. It went soul deep.

Death smiled, the expression making Cami's stomach drop.

It's beginning.

No going back now.

Next to her, Liam's breath hitched, and she managed to draw her gaze from the foursome to find him staring at War, some kind of recognition flaring in his dark eyes.

It didn't matter. She had to focus. She turned back as Death spoke, "Enjoy your last night of indulgence, my friends. The morning will find you in much less comfortable circumstances." She motioned and a picture appeared on the wall behind her. It was a satellite image of the Island of Ys. The smaller one looked a little like a crab, it's pinchers extending to create the bay both casinos and the boardwalk edged up against. The larger island was more crescent shaped. It housed some beaches, what looked to be cliffs, and much higher rolling hills.

And jungle. Lots and lots of jungle.

"Capture the White Stag within the seven-day time period and the prize is yours. Fail ..." She shrugged. "Murder is not expressly condoned, but it's a risk you take by participating. The White Stag will have a twelve-hour head start on you, but they will be entering the island with the same materials allowed the competitors. Limited rations. Water filter. A knife. A beacon that, when triggered, will be an automatic disqualification and an immediate extraction."

Cami noticed she didn't say appropriate clothing. The sinking in her stomach got worse. On the surface, this seemed like every other Wild Hunt the Horsemen had hosted in the past, but she couldn't shake the suspicion that another shoe was about to drop.

Death didn't make her wait long.

"This year, however, is special. Our dearest War has proven herself more than a match for anyone who tries to best her." There it was again, that cat-with-the-canary smile. "As such, we've decided to even the playing field." Her dark gaze landed on Cami, the only warning she got before Death said, "And that's why Princess Camilla Fitzcharles will play the part of White Stag in this year's hunt."

Cami gripped the table in front of her, fighting against the sensation of falling. She kept her chin up, kept her gaze on Death. Even as she promised herself she wouldn't do it, she looked at Luca, dreading finding a glare or a superior expression there.

All she saw was shock.

Shock and a growing rage.

He moved to Death, grabbing her arm and speaking low in her ear. Whatever she said back was lost in the low murmur of the room. Death leaned back and looked at the spot where he held her with such menace that Luca dropped his hand. She turned back to the room, reclaiming her smile. "As in years' past, the betting will open at midnight. Good luck, my friends."

War wove through the tables and extended her hand to Cami. "Let's go."

Because she'd need every second of head start to keep away from the people hunting her. Cami took the woman's hand with numb fingers, allowing herself to be tugged to her feet. She could feel the eyes of everyone in the room on her, but it was nothing like before. They studied her for weakness, for something to exploit, for the key to unlock her—and their win.

Even Liam, with his gruff smile and sweet introduction, was doing it.

They would cut her down, and they wouldn't think twice about it. She knew that. Of course she'd known that. But it felt different when they were all still on the same playing field, all still hunters.

Now Cami was undeniably the prey.

War didn't speak until they were inside Cami's villa. "Change while I talk. You don't have much time."

Twelve hours could be a small eternity in certain scenarios, but the people hunting her were all highly motivated to see her taken down. Twelve hours was barely a drop in the ocean.

Cami threw herself into motion. She stripped out of the gown and pulled out the backpack she'd put together before she left Thalania. It wasn't large as such things went, only containing the allowed items and a change of clothes. She pulled on a pair of pants, boots, a sports bra and a tank top. The nights didn't get particularly cold this time of year, but she had a jacket stashed just in case. She walked out of her room to find War waiting for her.

The blonde took her in. "Okay, good. I was hoping you'd be at least a little prepared." She worried her bottom lip. "Look, it's nothing personal. Or, well, it's *mostly* not personal. Death has her reasons."

Somehow, that didn't make Cami feel the least bit better. She lifted her chin. "If I avoid them for the full seven days, I win the favor." *I win my freedom.*

Sympathy flared in War's amber eyes. "You can try, little princess."

She shouldn't ask. Her mantra of *show no weakness* demanded she keep silent. But Cami couldn't stop the words from falling from her lips. "Did Luca know?"

"Does it matter?"

"Yes." No hesitation there. He wanted her gone from the island, and she had to know if he tried to shuttle her away because he knew the danger she'd be in. If he'd coaxed her to bring herself to orgasm on his hand just a few hours ago knowing what would happen next.

War sighed. "I should lie to you and put everyone out of their misery, but I love an underdog. It's one of my many charms." She nudged Cami toward the door. "No, little princess. He didn't know. He found out you'd play the White Stag the moment you did."

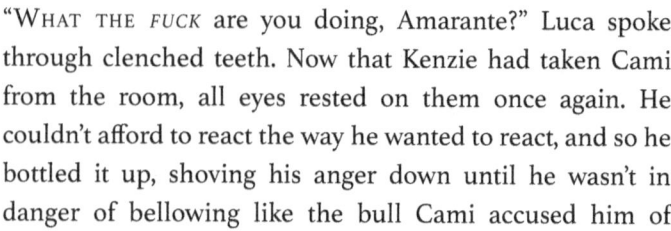

"WHAT THE *FUCK* are you doing, Amarante?" Luca spoke through clenched teeth. Now that Kenzie had taken Cami from the room, all eyes rested on them once again. He couldn't afford to react the way he wanted to react, and so he bottled it up, shoving his anger down until he wasn't in danger of bellowing like the bull Cami accused him of being.

Amarante sighed, the exhale nearly soundless. "Not here."

"Then you'd better walk your ass out of this room if you want to avoid making a scene."

She turned with a practiced smile to the competitors. "Enjoy your meal. We'll speak more afterward." Amarante led the way through the door. Ryu still hadn't spoken, but that was typical Ryu. He would follow Amarante right into hell if she asked it of him.

They all would.

But not *this*. Luca hadn't signed on for making a sacrificial lamb of an innocent.

Of Cami.

Amarante didn't speak again until they'd reached the hub. "I knew you'd react like this."

"You know, it's funny that you knew I'd react like this, so you kept it from me *and did it anyway*."

She spun on him and propped her hands on her narrow hips. "I'm killing two birds with one stone, Luca. We need Kenzie onsite in order to accomplish the first step of this plan, and that means someone else has to play the part of the White Stag. It can't be you or Ryu. I have my own part to play in this thing."

Her words rang of the truth, but not the full truth. "And the rest?"

There it was, the fury she kept so carefully banked most of the time. It flared in her dark eyes, hot enough to burn them all alive. "Thalania has a problem taking no for an answer. First the Nibley delegation, then the king himself. Now this princess? No." She shook her head, black hair swinging. "You made your choice, and if they won't respect it, then I'll shove that answer down their goddamn throats."

Realization rolled over him. "You're making an example of her." If she was someone else, if the situation were different ... But it wasn't. "Not her, Amarante. She may be a thorn in our sides, but she doesn't deserve to be crushed."

"That's no longer your call to make." She shrugged. "She's already gone."

He went still. They had disagreements over the years. It would be impossible for four such strong personalities to maintain their relationship without things coming to a head from time to time. He'd never wanted to cut all ties with them as much as he did in that moment. "You crossed a line. We have rules for a reason."

Amarante dropped her hands and glared at him. "Oh no you don't. There are times when I deserve to be painted as the villain, and this may be one of them, but that girl came here of her own free will. She *insisted* on joining the Hunt despite my making it exceptionally difficult for her. I did not go tempting innocent princesses into playing this game, and I sure as hell didn't abduct one. You even tried to get her to leave. How did that go over?"

Not particularly well, which she was obviously aware of.

It didn't make him any less angry at his sister. "You could have chosen someone else."

"I'm not going to apologize for this. It was the right call. You might not see it now, but you will eventually."

When this was all over.

Luca turned away from her and scrubbed his hands over his face. He just had to *think*, but all he could picture was the horrible shit that could happen to Cami on that island. If the local wildlife didn't cause problems, there were traps and pits and a thousand different ways to end up injured— or worse. The competitors only added to the danger. Catching the White Stag wasn't enough. They had to transfer her to one of the extraction locations in order to win. Kenzie had even had some close calls in the past and she was the most capable of all of them for this kind of challenge.

Cami wouldn't stand a chance.

"I'm going after her." The declaration burst from him, but as the words fell between them, they felt right. He wasn't a good man, but he wasn't capable of sitting idly by and watching someone like Cami go through hell.

A strange sort of relief filtered through him. *I still have lines I won't cross.*

"Luca." Amarante's tone stopped him in his tracks.

He turned slowly to face her. "This is wrong, Te."

"I'm not going to apologize for protecting us."

"I don't expect you to." She'd earned that much and more from him. From all of them. "But I'm still going after her."

She didn't so much as blink. "You're running the risk of jeopardizing a decade's worth of work. If there is no Wild Hunt, then the Bookkeeper has no reason to come here. We won't be able to find the trail back to its source. We won't be able to find the ones responsible."

Damn it. *Damn it.*

She was right. He knew she was right. But how the fuck was he supposed to choose between the monster who had terrorized them for far too long and the woman who didn't deserve any of this?

The fact he even weighed Cami in the balance told him things he'd rather not think about, but he couldn't seem to smother the instinct to go after her. If he chose their quest for justice over her and something happened … He'd never forgive himself. "I can't just sit here and watch."

Amarante nodded. "There's a spot open among the competitors now. If you're going after her, then that's how you do it." She gave a sad little smile. "It may even sweeten the pot for our enemies. They'd commit unforgivable acts for a chance to take you out of the picture."

"I'll do it." Three little words to seal his fate.

"There are conditions." When he gave her a look, she raised her brows. "Come now, Luca, you know better. You can't go sprinting in there and spirit her to safety. You can compete, but you *can't* win. Everything rides on this."

He might not have played White Stag the same way Kenzie had in the past, but he knew that island almost as well as she did. The camera locations, the traps, the secret spaces no one outside the Horsemen knew about. Luca wasn't sure it would be enough, but it'd have to do. "I want to keep her safe, Te. She didn't know what she was asking for."

"You're underestimating her." She moved to the wall of monitors and typed a set of commands in that had it switching over to the camera situated on the western docks. The network there wasn't as large as the eastern ones that were nestled in the bay, their purpose more for internal use than for guests. He moved closer to the monitor, watching as Kenzie drove up in one of their carts, Cami in the passenger seat.

She didn't *look* terrified out of her mind, but she had to be scared. This wasn't how things were supposed to go for her. The woman had a plan, and they'd just burned it to ash around her. Luca found himself clenching his fists and forced his hands to relax. "I won't win."

"You have to let them catch her—and you can't be seen helping her."

He spun around. "Are you out of your fucking mind?"

Amarante stared him down. "You have to let them catch her," she repeated. "The Bookkeeper has to win, Luca. If you can't handle that, I'll tranq you and lock you in your room for the duration of the Hunt. Agree to the terms or you're not getting on that boat."

"What if she wins?"

Amarante laughed. "Funny."

It might be possible with Kenzie bending the rules, but she was right—Cami would be caught, and likely caught early. As it was, he'd be hard pressed to get to her before the others.

She shrugged. "Statistically, the Bookkeeper's people have better odds of finding her than anyone else."

He'd read the files. None of the other three were likely to hurt Cami if they caught her first. Subdue? Definitely. Torment and worse? No way. But the Bookkeeper's people? Their files were filled with the kind of shit that would give people nightmares. He couldn't let them get their hands on the princess. "Fine, Te. I'll let them win."

"You'll *ensure* they win."

Luca stared. "You've got to be fucking with me."

"I'm not."

The brilliance of her plan had him wanting to curse and praise her in dual measures. He might have done the latter if she wasn't guilty of manipulating *him*. "We're not supposed to play games with each other. That's not how we work."

Amarante stalked to the monitors, turned on one spike red heel, and stalked back. "Plans change, Luca. We have to be adaptable." She drew herself up, the same way she always had before stepping into the ring. "I didn't know you'd have a soft spot for the girl. Kenzie was supposed to be the one to step into the empty competitor position. I didn't tell you because you didn't need to know. I wasn't playing games with *you*."

"And yet here we are."

"And yet here we are," she echoed. "Will you trust Kenzie to play her part?"

He'd trusted Kenzie with his life and sanity and more. She and Amarante were the sisters he hadn't been born with, the family created from fire and pain and trauma beyond knowing. A week ago, if she'd asked him this same question, he would have answered an affirmative without question.

Now?

Now he couldn't be sure.

There were only three people in this world Amarante held loyalty to, and Cami didn't number among them. If it came down to a choice between Cami and their plan, Amarante might spare a moment of regret, but she'd sacrifice Cami without a second thought. Kenzie would act in an extension of that will.

He couldn't risk it. Luca took a slow breath. There was only one way out of this, and it was through. "I'll be a good boy and play by your rules."

She hesitated, something unsure passing over her face. "Luca ... I don't know if it helps or hurts at this point, but I really didn't think you'd be this invested in the girl. She's here to force you back to the family who lost you. I assumed you'd feel the same way about her that you have about every other representative Thalania has sent."

"We both know it doesn't make a damn bit of difference how I feel. Not at the end of the day."

"I'm trying to keep us safe." Words she'd used to justify so much over the years. Words he'd never questioned.

He didn't question them now. Amarante would always do what it took to keep them safe, no matter how reprehensible the act. He'd never judged her for that. He fought not to judge her for it now.

He'd have to take a page from her book. To keep Cami safe long enough to send her back to where she came from. Any other outcome was unthinkable.

6

The island looked so much larger up close. Cami stood next to War on the boat as it cut through the narrow strip of ocean separating the resort island from this one. Neither of them spoke. What was there to say? She was the White Stag, and she had a mere twelve hours to figure out a game plan and start to follow through on it.

Twelve hours before the other competitors began hunting her.

War guided their boat to a beach partially sheltered by a series of large rectangular rocks. They were a feature this series of islands were known for, and Cami had found them unexpectedly charming in photographs. Now, with night fully set and only the light of the moon illuminating them, they looked like sentinels warning the unwary traveler from landing there.

Unfortunately, this traveler didn't have a choice.

War eased off the throttle and let them coast onto the gently sloped beach. "This is our stop."

"I'd say thanks, but ..."

"But you kind of want to kick my ass right now. Yeah, I get it." War leaned on the steering wheel and blew out a breath. "Look, between you, me, and the island, I'm actually a little sorry about this. You seem like you're not completely trash, and that makes this a little harder than I expected."

"Thanks?"

"Oh, yeah, that was definitely a compliment." War hefted the backpack and passed it to Cami. "Word of advice. We drop the competitors at different spots along the coast. They'll expect you to go for high ground, so that's where most of them will head to start."

Cami looked at the high hills she could barely make out against the canopy of stars overhead. "If I stay on the coast, that means they just have to catch me and hold me there until the pickup comes."

"Only two locations they can signal a pickup from. This beach." She pointed to the one they currently occupied. "And one tucked down in the cliffs on the south-west side of the island."

"Seems risky."

"Little princess, everything about this game is risky. You'll take your chances wherever you are headed." War looked up at the moon and something about her softened, as if the glowing crescent in the sky smoothed away her sharp edges. "I'm not going to lie, I'm a little bummed out not to play hare to their hounds this year. It's nice to shuck off the niceties every once and awhile."

Cami didn't know how to respond to that. She had never shucked off the niceties. Not truly. Even when she'd left palace life behind, when she was training with Yael, there were still rules to follow, expectations laid over her. She moved to the front of the boat and hopped down to the sand. "I guess I'll see you on the other side."

"If someone doesn't murder you first." War laughed. "Sorry, gallows humor. Happy hunting, little princess. And may the odds be ever in your favor." With that downright depressing quote, she kicked the engine back into gear and guided the boat off the beach.

Cami didn't stick around to watch her leave. The clock in her mind ticked down, and panic fluttered in her throat. Seven days to avoid capture. A week. An amount of time that could fly by between one blink and the next, or stretch out until a person was sure it'd never end.

She already knew which category this one would fall into.

As tempting as it was to sprint into the jungle and put as much distance between herself and the pick-up point, there were other factors to consider. The place was riddled with traps. Some of them were pits, some cleverly concealed cages, others fell into a variety of categories. When she'd first decided she wanted to compete in the Wild Hunt, she'd spent some time digging through the dark web for footage of past Hunts. The dangers differed from year to year, but every competition, at least half of the competitors were taken out by the traps. Kenzie, of course, evaded them with ease, but she also had the advantage of knowing where they were.

Cami forced herself to stop. To plan.

She'd have to sleep eventually. Adrenaline only maintained her energy level for so long, and she'd be vulnerable when she finally gave in to exhaustion. That must be taken into account.

Come on. You had a strategy for this Hunt.

Yeah, but it was designed to find and contain War, not to evade people trying to find and contain *her*.

Adapt or die, Cami. Adapt or die.

When laid out like that, there was no other option.

Cami pictured the island in her head, tracing the western curve where the beaches morphed into cliffs. If she went that way, she'd be trapped. The only relief in the western cliffs was the low beach that served as an extraction point. The eastern shore was mostly beaches, but the large rock formations were littered throughout. It was possible to take War's advice, stick to the coast, and potentially hide there. If she found a good spot before the competitors were delivered to the island, she might be able to prepare and hide until they moved farther inland.

After that, she'd have to play it by ear.

Not a foolproof plan by any definition of the word, but it was better than nothing. The jungle might be attractive in theory—more places to hide, more cover—but the same things that could benefit her were just as likely to hinder her. She couldn't risk it. Not this early in the game.

Cami hitched her backpack more firmly onto her shoulders and started south.

"WE KNEW YOU WERE A BITCH, Death, but we never figured you for a cheat."

Luca glared at the man who'd just spoken—one of the Bookkeeper's representatives, Dolph Richardson. He was a massive guy, and scars wrapped around the side of his head, speaking to a life spent in the trenches of violence and crime. The man noted his attention and gave him a slow grin. "Though I wouldn't be too sad to take out Famine. Don't you think so, boys?"

The two men at his back exchanged glances, but didn't say anything. In fact, *no one* except Dolph had said anything since Amarante announced that Luca would take Cami's place in the competition.

Amarante gave Dolph a bored look. "Your protest has been noted."

"And?"

"I'm sorry, were you expecting a pat on the back? You don't make the rules here, Mr. Richardson. We do. Since War is no longer representing our interests in the form of the White Stag, it's only right that Famine ensures you are all playing your best game." Her lips drew up in a smile that made Dolph flinch. "Unless you feel you aren't up to the task?"

"I never said that!"

"Good, then we're in agreement." She swept her attention through the room. "Unless anyone else has an objection?"

The assassin, Envy, spoke, her melodious voice seeming to fill the room. "In the unlikely event that the princess evades capture, does that result in a win for her?"

"Yes." Another of Amarante's cold smiles. "If she's still free by sunset of the seventh day, she will win the promised favor. I'm sure that's an impossible feat with such a ... qualified ... group of competitors, don't you?"

Envy didn't answer, instead turning to speak with her companion. Luca couldn't be sure, but he thought she might be Lust. Nothing in Envy's dossier had given any indication if she'd be in her element in this kind of competition—her special brand was mimicking other's murders in a perfect copycat—but he couldn't imagine she'd sign up without being sure she was capable of winning.

He put it from his mind.

Dolph was right to be pissed Luca had entered the competition. He knew that island. As far as they were aware, he was there to ensure none of them won the favor Amarante offered as a prize. What remained to be seen was whether the temptation to knock him out of the game completely was enough to quell their protests.

Amarante nodded. "You'll be collected from your villas at six tomorrow morning. After being searched to ensure you're in compliance with the rules, you'll be transported to your individual drop-off point. Let the games begin." She turned and walked through the door, Ryu falling into step behind her.

Dolph walked up, his chest out, his legs stiff as if he were a junkyard dog about to attack. "Playing this game is going to be the worst mistake you ever made, Famine."

Famine. The persona he wore when facing the outside world. Only three people called him by his given name. There were a handful of people in Thalania who knew who he was, where he came from, but they kept the knowledge close to their chests. Losing a potential heir to one of their noble Families wasn't a good look. Losing him, only to have him turn up later as one of the Four Horsemen?

Yeah, they had their reasons for keeping their mouths shut.

He met the other man's gaze steadily. "Time will tell."

"Do you think Death will mourn your loss?" Dolph looked over his shoulder as his cronies. "Maybe I'll have to comfort her afterward."

Luca gave himself a full ten seconds imagining what would be left of Dolph's body after Amarante got through with him. A ruin. Something barely identifiable as human.

No one went to Amarante's bed without her explicit permission, and in all the time they'd known each other, he could number on one hand how many times it had happened and still have fingers left over. All four of them carried scars from their time in hell, and they each had their own way of dealing with the nightmares that followed them through the years. Kenzie became *more*, extra outlandish in her determination to grasp life with both hands and never let go. Ryu withdrew, preferring to keep a shield between him and the rest of the world. Amarante craved control as much as she craved vengeance.

Luca?

He carved off pieces of himself in order to stay on his feet, to keep moving forward. He kept people at a distance, because he could trust no one. A betrayal of the highest order landed him in hell, and he'd never make that mistake again. Ever.

He forced himself out of the past and into the present. What had Dolph said? Ah, yes. Luca smiled. "I may crawl out of my grave just to see how that works out for you, Dolph." Before the other man could dredge up a response, he turned and walked away.

There was no point in chatting with anyone else in the room. He knew their strengths, just like he knew their weaknesses. Luca headed back to the hub, his past nipping at his heels. This Hunt wouldn't be easy. Kenzie might find freedom away from civilization, but that wasn't Luca's path. The opulence of the little island might strain him at times, but it didn't remind him of what he'd survived.

Going to the big island would.

It didn't matter that the jungle and ocean and beaches were nothing like the pine trees and mud of that place. It was still closer than he ever wanted to get to hell again.

He ignored Ryu's questioning gaze as he walked through the hub to his private quarters. Twelve hours until the Hunt began wasn't much preparation time, but he had a permanent bag packed. A weakness, a testament that he didn't quite believe the safety Amarante had woven around them, but they all had their ways of coping. Luca knew he could grab his bag and run at a second's notice and so he was able to sleep. End of story.

He dumped it onto his bed and went through the process of repacking, leaving out the things that were forbidden during the Hunt. No guns, no weapons of any kind aside from a single knife. After the first year of having some idiot try to justify a machete as a knife, they'd put clear size restrictions on the blade allowed. He picked up his and slid it out of the sheath. The blade was matte black, so it wouldn't shine in the light and give his position away in the dark. He set it aside. It would go in the holster at his waist, rather than the pack.

A spare set of clothes, extra socks, MREs, a water filter and a canteen.

The big island held secrets the competitors didn't know about, secrets he had to be careful he didn't reveal. But the knowledge served as an ace up his sleeve. He might have agreed to Amarante's terms, but he would ensure that Cami remained safe. No matter what.

Luca expected the knock on his door, but he still tensed at the sound. "Yeah?"

Ryu stepped into the room and leaned against the door-frame. "You good?"

"I'm fine."

"Uh huh." Ryu tilted his head to the side, examining Luca as if he'd never seen him before. "Not like you to let someone get under your skin, let alone so fast."

No, it wasn't. He couldn't explain it, either. It was more than wanting to fuck Cami, though he'd be a liar if he said the desire didn't exist. The thought of her being hurt made him sick to his stomach. He wasn't even sure he liked her, but she didn't move in the same world they did. She might not be a complete innocent—after fucking his hand on the beach, he couldn't quite keep the label attached—but she was *innocent*. He couldn't allow her to be mercilessly used, no matter how it served their endgame. There had to be lines Luca wouldn't cross. This was one of them.

Ryu still waited for an answer, so he said, "She doesn't deserve to be hurt because of this—because of me."

"Your armor's a little tarnished to go chasing after damsels to save, don't you think?" Ryu shook his head. "It's a moot point. She's more capable than you're giving her credit for."

"How would you know?"

Ryu gave him the look that question deserved. Ryu knew *everything*. His skill with computers bordered on magical, and he comforted himself with knowledge the same way Luca comforted himself with his bug out bag. Ryu pushed off the door frame. "She might surprise you."

"No matter how capable she is, she's out of her element in this Hunt. She'll get hurt."

Ryu shrugged. "Guess we'll see." He turned. "The bets are rolling in faster than they have in all the past Hunts combined. Your girl is looking at 73-3 odds."

"She's not my girl." The protest came too quickly, too harshly. It made a liar of him.

Another of those infuriating shrugs. "Guess we'll see about that, too." Ryu walked away.

Luca loved his siblings, his chosen family, a whole hell of a lot. Some days he still wanted to throttle all three of them. He turned back to his bag and went through it again, ensuring he was as prepared as he possibly could be. After that, there was nothing left to do but catch some sleep.

He lay down and stilled his racing mind through sheer

force of will. Luca had never seen combat in the traditional sense of the word, but he acquired the skill of being able to sleep anywhere, in any given condition, the same way many soldiers did. He closed his eyes, and between one inhale and the next, he was out.

Only to be shaken awake what felt like seconds later by Kenzie. She wore a pair of black jeans and a slinky shirt that seemed like it was more straps than actual fabric. "Get up, lazybones."

"You're one to talk." He groaned and sat up. "If you didn't want to play in the jungle, you should have said so instead of tossing someone out there in your place."

"Yeah, yeah, you can be pissed at me later. We need to move. If you miss the boat to the big island, then you're shit out of luck."

He pulled on his boots, grabbed his bag, and followed her. There was no sign of Amarante or Ryu in the hub, but he hadn't expected them to show up. Goodbyes were just an invitation for fate to make sure a person never returned home. He knew how they felt about him, just like they knew how he felt about them. No reason for emotional bullshit and prolonged farewells.

He'd be back inside a week.

Luca ignored the uneasiness the thought brought. No matter what he'd told himself up to this point, this wasn't a simple mission. Maybe if he could have charged over there, hauled Cami to one of the extraction points, and finished this inside of twenty-four hours. But Amarante had hamstrung him with her conditions. He could keep Cami safe, but he had to make sure it didn't look like he was doing it for the cameras.

He had to ensure one of the Bookkeeper's people won.

That last one would be the most difficult. It meant at

some point, she'd be completely outside Luca's safety net, completely at the mercy of those fuckers. He could shadow them, could maybe save her from the worst of it, but Luca would have his hands tied.

She'd never forgive him.

He gave himself a shake. Who gave a fuck if she didn't forgive him? He wasn't leaving the island, and he had every intention of putting her ass on the next chopper out the second the Hunt was over. Cami was a woman built for the protected life she enjoyed back in Thalania. Her brother, the king, might even be so grateful to have her returned, he'd leave Luca the fuck alone.

The whole plan rang a little flat, but he ignored that, too. The future wasn't a given. The only thing he could control was what would happen on that island. He'd worry about the rest later.

"Luca?" Kenzie's tone said this wasn't the first time she'd spoken.

"Yeah?"

"Be careful, okay? I know I make that shit look easy, but the big island is no joke. Don't let your girl be the reason you get your ass handed to you."

He slowed. "I'll be okay."

"You better. If I have to cut my way through the Book-keeper's people to avenge your death, Amarante will throw my ass in one of Pain's deprivation tanks for ruining our plans."

He pulled Kenzie into a rough hug. "I'm coming back. I promise."

"I'll hold you to that." She nudged him back and, just like that, all vulnerability was gone from her face, replaced by a saucy grin. "Let's get your ass on that boat!"

ami pressed herself against the side of the rock as a boat motor cut through the early morning air. She hadn't made quite as good time as she would have liked, but the terrain was more challenging than she'd expected. The large rock outcroppings meant she had to skirt inland time and time again to get around them. The jungle was also thick enough in places that she would have done unforgivable things to get her hands on a machete instead of the six-inch knife she'd been allowed.

Now here she was, hiding like a fox as the hounds circled.

She closed her eyes. *No. I am not defenseless.* It just felt that way in that moment, with her crouched down and listening to the boat cruise closer. They must be aiming for the beach just south of her, a couple of meters away. She kept still as the boat stopped. Two people spoke, but between the motor and the distance, she couldn't make out their words. Only when the boat retreated again did Cami risk a look.

It was one of the only other women competitors. Not the

pretty Hispanic assassin. No, this was the one who'd been part of the larger alliance. Her dark skin already shone with sweat and though she moved with purpose, she seemed to be cursing the sand getting into her boots already.

Cami did some quick calculations. If this competitor was dropped here, the other six must be roughly equidistance around the island. *Wait a minute, you can't afford to assume that.* They might be lining them up on the east side of the island, which would make Cami avoiding them all nearly impossible.

She could simply stay there and wait for them to move inland and then resume her path south. It was probably the safest bet. They would expect her to rabbit, and they would plan their pursuit accordingly. When they looked at her, all they saw was prey. A little girl playing with the big bad villains.

A victim in waiting.

She shifted down the rock a little to get a better look at the competitor. The woman had reached the end of the beach, was looking at the jungle encroaching on the sand as if it might reach out and take a swipe out of her. *Scared.* She was scared of the dark green world she stood on the edge of.

Apparently the prize from catching Cami was too tempting, though. She took a visible fortifying breath and charged into the green.

She leaned back with a sigh. That woman wouldn't last long in the trees. She'd make some excuse and circle back to the beach. A quick look at Cami's watch told her that the true heat of the day was just beginning. As much as the white sandy beaches felt like paradise when she was in a bikini and stretched out on a lounge chair, right now it represented a special kind of hell. She needed cover from the sun, and she wasn't going to get it here amongst these rocks, even though a few of them were taller than she was.

What to do?

Frustration bubbled up beneath her skin. This wasn't part of the plan, wasn't what she signed up for, definitely wasn't the big break she needed to finally secure her independence. No, it was just Princess Cami again, the helpless little girl who couldn't stand on her own two feet.

Stop that.

She was here. No, that didn't look like she'd thought it would, but she made it all the same. She had to remain free the next seven days ...

Cami went still.

Wait a damn minute. The competitors had to find her and transport her to an extraction site. That's it. Those were the only rules of this game.

There were absolutely no rules saying *she* couldn't neutralize *the competitors*.

She grinned for the first time since Death announced her playing the White Stag. It was a risk to seek the competitors out. They were here because they were the best—and had the deepest pockets. She couldn't afford to underestimate the hunters, and she certainly wouldn't be able to overpower nearly any of them.

She had to outsmart them. There were traps all over this island. If Cami could find them and trap the competitors, one by one, she might have a chance of winning this thing after all.

She pulled her pack back on and climbed through the rock formation. Following directly in the woman's footsteps was too risky, but she could move parallel and shadow her. Once Cami found a trap, she could lure the woman in and remove her from the competition.

There are other ways to remove them.

Permanent ways.

She wasn't willing to take that course of action. Not yet. Not over a game. If she had to defend herself, that was one thing. Cami wasn't going to literally hunt the competition. Murder may be allowed on this island, but that didn't mean she'd suddenly turned into a killer overnight. Or that she even wanted to.

This hunt is sending you spiraling. Focus, Cami.

Right. Focus. First deal with this competitor and then figure out the next step.

Cami took a deep breath and melted into the jungle after the woman.

LUCA HATED THIS SHIT. He hated the sticky heat. He hated the bugs buzzing around his face. He hated the trees and vines that seemed determined to trip him up with every step. Even knowing he wouldn't get any special treatment, he'd still hoped for better than Kenzie's, "Figure it out, brother."

The only advantage Luca had was knowing Kenzie's past strategies and guessing that she might advise Cami, one White Stag to another. His sister would love that shit.

Kenzie always headed down the coast. Sometimes she looped up and around the north end of the island first, but he doubted Cami would make that choice. The western cliffs gave the impression of nowhere to go, and she'd want to keep her options open.

So here he was, in a different kind of hell than his past, searching for evidence of her trail.

She'd made it farther than he would have expected,

nearly halfway down the coast. At that point, she'd decided for some reason to cut inland. Luca stared at the tracks. They weren't as obvious as he would have expected, either. She'd purposefully moved around the softer dirt and sand and posted up on the rocks where it was harder to see if she'd been there.

Smart.

Really smart.

There was a time after they escaped from hell when his life had hung in the balance, dependent solely on his ability to track down animals for them to eat. In the weeks it took them to transverse the relative wilderness until they reached civilization, it was the only thing that kept them alive.

Fifteen years later, as much as he loathed it and what it represented, he couldn't control the compulsion to keep up on the skillset. Somewhere in the deepest, darkest part of his mind, he feared that all this could be taken from them. It didn't matter how many fortifications, literal and figurative, that they put up to prevent that very thing from happening. He'd had protections before, when he was still the pampered son of a Thalanian noble. Protections and security and a life designed to keep him safe.

It hadn't helped then.

He still wasn't convinced it would help now.

Christ, get a hold of yourself.

Easier said than done. The weight of the jungle pressed against his sanity, edging him closer to the precipice. Luca braced his hands against the rock formation and took several slow breaths. It didn't stop the sun or the pounding in his temples. It didn't cause his rising stress to suddenly disappear.

But his mind cleared, just a little.

Get Cami. Keep her safe until he could figure out how to

arrange one of the Bookkeeper's people to take her to the extraction point.

That was it. The whole goal.

This hunt would be over in seven short days. Less time if he could play his cards right.

Luca took another breath, made himself release the rock, and stepped into the trees. Instantly, the sun became half as strong, barely dappling through the heavy growth overhead. He looked around, forcing himself to note the differences between this forest and the one of his nightmares. No snow on the ground. No scent of pine in the air. No freezing air dry enough to cause a nosebleed. It didn't feel the same, not in any real way.

He could do this.

He kept moving, following signs of Cami's passing as she turned inland.

An hour later, he went still. There was someone up ahead. He looked around, trying to get his bearings. There were cameras located all over this island—the better to record the competitors and stir the wagers from the audience in the casino into a frenzy. If he found Cami, he had to ensure the cameras didn't pick up on his true motivations or the whole Hunt would be compromised. It would ruin everything, and it could potentially endanger her further in the process.

No one held grudges like the Bookkeeper and those he associated with.

Luca looked around and ultimately decided that the tree to his right was the best option. He scaled it easily and braced himself between two branches. On the other side of the tree, the ground dipped down into a shallow ravine. In that ravine stood Cami and the Bookkeeper's woman, Brianna, though he'd bet a significant amount of money that it wasn't her real name. She had the documents to back up her identity, but that sort of thing could be procured if one knew the right people. She did.

Brianna circled Cami, looking like a tiger playing with its next meal. *Because that's exactly what's happening.* Cami's backpack was long gone, and she looked particularly small and helpless in comparison to the other woman. She held out shaking hands, her face a mask of terror. "Please. Please don't. I can pay—"

Brianna charged. Luca tensed, but he was too far away to do anything. He tightened his grip on the branches, ready to launch himself down there, but Cami stepped neatly aside at the last moment. She planted two hands on Brianna's back and gave her an extra shove. The woman disappeared from view, a metal clang sounding through the clearing.

I'll be damned.

She just tricked Brianna into one of the many traps littering the island.

Cursing rose as Brianna must have realized her predicament. Cami shook her head sadly. "I did try to warn you." She walked to a tree half torn from the ground and retrieved her bag from its roots. She ... planned this.

Luca narrowed his eyes, seeing her for what felt like the first time. She'd used the woman's assumptions to get the best of her. No telling if it would work on the others, but she wasn't nearly as helpless as he'd believed.

Little Cami Fitzcharles held unknown depths and the skills to match.

He considered showing himself, but curiosity got the best of him. Was this just a one-off where she'd got lucky? Even as part of him analyzed the thought process that must have gone into this particular trap—finding the cage without falling victim to it, somehow drawing Brianna to her, baiting her into charging—Luca couldn't help looking for other explanations. She was capable, sure, but *this* capable? Surely it was just luck.

Kenzie would have pulled a move like that. She has *pulled moves like that in the past.*

But Cami and Kenzie couldn't have been more different. It defied explanation.

I underestimated her.

All that remained was to figure out his next step and how he wanted to play this.

SOMEONE WAS FOLLOWING HER.

Cami didn't look over her shoulder. She wouldn't see anything even if she moved quickly. Whoever it was had skills, and they moved nearly silently as they shadowed her steps. But she'd spent too much time training with Yael not to know when someone was hunting her.

She looked up, trying to gauge how long before sunset. By her watch's time, there should be hours left yet, but the whole area looked distinctly dimmer than it had even an hour ago. *The tree are playing tricks.* She couldn't risk moving after dark. Finding that trap earlier had been a gift, but even with actively looking for it, she'd nearly fallen into the thing. If she couldn't see well? She was just as likely to end up in a cage as to trick someone else into it.

No, better to find somewhere to camp out now while she still had light left.

Cami stopped and looked around slowly. She was relatively familiar with the area after all the research she'd done, but this place was just so *different* from Thalania. No matter how much preparing she did, a gap still remained from what she was familiar with and what she was experiencing.

Chin up, Cami. There are only six competitors left.

Only.

She almost laughed. She might be able to spin the men's perception of her enough to trick them ... as long as they hadn't teamed up. Four of those guys had seemed awfully cozy, and even as confident in her abilities as she was, there were limits to what she could accomplish.

Cami turned for the beach again. Everything was so wet in the jungle, she wasn't sure she could start a fire—or if she even should. At least if she could get a good spot in the rock formations, it would hide the light of her fire from anyone looking. They'd have to all but stumble on her to find her location.

In theory.

So much of what she operated on was theory right now.

Her skin prickled and she shivered. Someone was *definitely* watching her, and she didn't think it was the cameras hidden around the island. She'd watched the videos of past years. The camera network was impressive, but hardly exhaustive. It was set up more like game cameras that hunters used—human-sized motion would turn them on and start recording.

No, it wasn't cameras watching her now.

It was a person.

She feigned tripping and used the motion to slip her knife out of its sheath. It had been over an hour, and if they intended to try to take her, they should have done it by now. Attack, subdue, begin the journey of transporting her to an extraction point.

The fact they stalked her meant ...

Nothing good.

Nothing good for *her*, at least.

Cami kept her movement loose and fluid as she climbed over an intricate root network and considered her options. She hadn't found another trap, and this person showed no signs of the kind of impulsiveness the woman had displayed earlier. They had to be waiting for the cover of night to attack, which meant she needed her camp set up sooner, rather than later.

They'd come for her with the darkness, and she'd be ready when they did.

8

Luca followed her as far as the beach, but he didn't leave the trees. The sand and rocks offered little cover for this kind of thing, and he wasn't interested in being found out yet. The temptation to simply watch over her was strong enough to have him reconsidering his options. If he could find the other competitors and take most of them out, then he could narrow the field extensively. The faster this was over, the better the chance of getting her out of here unscathed.

Or at least avoiding any permanent harm.

Luca waited until she disappeared into the rocks and climbed down from the tree he'd perched in. He knew where they dropped competitors in past games, so there was no reason they'd use different drop points just because he was involved. If anything, Kenzie and Amarante wanted to avoid any accusations of playing favorites. They'd do things exactly as they'd always been done.

In the half day since they'd landed on the island, though, the others could be anywhere. Most of the time they moved inland. Even though the island wasn't particularly large—about ten miles north to south and fewer than five at its thickest point—that still left a lot of ground to cover.

All the while, Cami would be left on her own.

He rubbed his hand against his sternum. A risk, and not a small one. If he made the wrong call, she'd pay the price of it.

Luca shook his head. No, it was better to just keep on his original path. Watch Cami, deal with any competitors that showed up as needed.

It was a shame she'd removed Brianna so neatly. She was the only one of the Bookkeeper's people that Luca would have wanted to win. At least then it lessened the chance of her attempting some violent act against Cami.

Call it what it is, Luca. Rape. You saw the way some of those men looked at Cami, and you're scared out of your fucking mind that they'll try to hurt her like that.

He clenched his fists and tried to focus. Imagining a worst-case scenario wouldn't do anyone any good. He had to take his chances and approach her now before they got too deep into this game. Offer his protection. Promise to let her win if she'd only let him keep her safe.

Lie.

Luca ran his hands over his face. Better to break her trust than let one of them break her body. Her spirit. She'd get over not winning the game—she wasn't going to be able to pull it off anyway. That trick she'd managed against Brianna was impressive, but Brianna was the least of the competitors. One of the others would get to her.

He was making the right call, damn it.

No matter how shitty it felt.

Luca waited for full dark before he made his move. The

lack of light would impede everyone on the island, and that meant they had a sliver of time before they had to worry about another competitor finding Cami. Best to use it to get this agreement put in place between them.

He stalked out of the trees and climbed up the rocks in the same direction she'd gone. He found her camp quickly, a small fire set up in the space between four of the towering rock formations. *Smart. The rocks will hide the flames.* She must be exhausted from the events of the day, because she was already in her sleeping bag, her little body curled up toward the top.

Something warm and uncomfortable sprang into Luca's chest. He rubbed the back of his hand against it, as if he could smooth it away. He should have known better. He cared whether this woman was safe. He wasn't sure he liked her all that much, but he didn't want to see her hurt.

It had been so long since he'd had something pure to protect.

Hell, he'd *never* had something pure to protect.

Everything touched by his world was tainted in its own way. Even him. *Especially* him. Cami wasn't scarred and battered and beaten, and he held the dubious honor of being the only thing standing in the way of that. He *had* to keep her safe.

He climbed down to the camp and hesitated. Would waking her scare her? Sitting here watching her sleep might be satisfying in the extreme, but he didn't think she'd appreciate that. Luca cursed himself for his sudden indecisive streak and bent down to shake Cami awake.

She chose that moment to strike.

He had half a second to process the fact that the lump in the sleeping back was *clothes* and then she took him to the ground, attacking from above. He fought back on instinct, striking up to dislodge her, but Cami dodged and shoved her knife against his throat. "Don't move."

Luca froze. She wouldn't cut his throat, would she? Surely not. But then, he hadn't thought she'd pull off an ambush like this, either.

Clearly, he'd underestimated Princess Cami Fitzcharles.

Again.

He slowly relaxed against the ground, holding his arms wide. "Since when do you know how to fight?"

"You don't get to ask the questions right now." Her hair stood half on end, like she'd dragged her fingers through it repeatedly, and her blue eyes held more than a little fury. "What are you doing out here?"

"Trying to wake you up."

"I know what you were doing *right here*. I want to know what you're doing on the island." She glared. "Does your group always cheat on these games?"

Yes, but he wasn't about to admit it. "I'm here because they needed another competitor spot filled." It wasn't the truth in the strictest sense of the word, but if he admitted that he was worried about her, it would pave the way toward things Luca wasn't ready to deal with. Expectations. Strings.

He might have misjudged her capabilities, but he hadn't misjudged *that*.

Cami was the kind of woman who made a man think settling down thoughts. Marriage. A family. Security of the like that Luca had never known. Impossible things.

What the fuck was he even thinking?

He protected her because she needed protection. End of story. It didn't matter how sweetly she came against his hand or how the stubborn tilt of her head drove him batshit crazy. When the Hunt ended, he'd ensure she made it back to the safety of her country, and he'd never see her again.

The edge of the knife bit into his skin, just a little. "I asked you a question," she said mildly.

"I answered."

"You lied."

Well, yeah. He raised his brows. "Are you planning on holding that knife on me all night?" Now that the immediate danger had passed, the fact that she straddled him was starting to register. He couldn't hide his body's response without moving, and she'd already proven herself willing to cut him.

Instead of getting flustered, she snorted. "Don't get any kinky ideas, Luca. I want answers, and I want them now. Why are you here?"

He wasn't getting out of this. If she was the kind of woman to be swayed, they wouldn't be in this situation to begin with. He huffed out a breath. "You're going to get your ass killed."

She blinked. "What?"

"You think this Hunt is a game, and while that's true in the technical sense of the word, those people out there tracking you aren't good people. Some of them are better than others, but that's not saying much. A full half of them would take their sweet time getting you to the extraction point because they'd want to enjoy you as their prize in the meantime."

Understanding flared in her blue eyes. "You'd allow that."

"*I* am not allowing shit. Neither is Amarante, or she wouldn't have approved me as a late edition to the Hunt." That, he believed. Amarante always had layers upon layers for doing something, and this situation wouldn't be the exception. Luca participating in the Hunt meant the competitors were distracted, and it meant she could influence the overall outcome. It also meant Cami wouldn't see any undo harm in the process.

Later he'd appreciate the nuances of her manipulations. Maybe.

"You expect me to believe that you're my protector?" She shook her head. "I don't think so."

This hadn't gone at all like he'd expected. Served him right for making assumptions. "Clearly you're more than capable of protecting yourself."

"Clearly." Her gaze dropped to his mouth and she tensed. "I'll let you up, but if you move wrong, I'm seriously considering stabbing you."

"Noted." He held perfectly still as she eased off him and retreated to her sleeping bag. Only then did Luca sit up and press a hand gingerly to his throat. She hadn't cut him deep, but she *had* cut him. "I wasn't aware that princesses came with this sort of skillset."

"You weren't aware of a lot of things." She methodically cleaned her knife with the ease of someone who'd done it many times before. Luca shifted back to lean against the nearest rock. It put him directly across the fire from her, and hell if the flickering light didn't make her even more attractive. Or maybe it was her clear ability to kick ass.

Cami replaced the knife in her sheath and looked at him. "Even if I believed you—and I don't—do you really think the betting pools and other sponsors will allow you to play guardian angel? You have to know they won't. *She* has to know they won't."

That, at least, he had an answer for. "I know where the cameras are and how to avoid them."

She didn't blink. "You have an answer for everything."

"Just let me *help* you."

Cami stared at him for another long moment, her

thoughts tucked away where he couldn't divine them. Finally, she shook her head. "No.

CAMI'S HANDS wouldn't stop shaking.

She'd almost killed Luca.

If her fear had gotten the better of her. If her hand had slipped in the tussle. If she hadn't recognized him in time. If, if, if. So many things could have gone wrong in the space of thirty seconds. She might have used his perceptions of her to get here, but she didn't want him *dead*.

Now he sat there and offered her help she desperately wanted to trust him enough to take. The island already felt safer with him sharing her fire, as if his standing between her and danger meant she really could win this Hunt.

She knew better.

Whatever his supposed reasons for being here, he wasn't telling Cami the full truth. And while she didn't necessarily think Death had it out for her, the level of supposed manipulation made Cami's head hurt. No way had the woman dispatched Luca as some kind of misguided guardian angel.

"Leave, please."

Luca stared at her like she'd grown a second head. "You aren't serious."

"I'm afraid so." It felt so strange to pull on court verbal skills when she was as far from the Thalanian palace as Cami had ever been, both physically and mentally. "I don't want or need your help. You're either a dangerous distraction, or you were placed here to ensure Death's outcome—which couldn't possibly favor me. Ergo, I don't want you anywhere close to me."

He lowered his brows. "I could just take you to the

extraction point myself. You might have gotten the drop on me, but you won't win in a fair fight."

Something she knew all too well. Which was why Cami had no intention of playing fair. "If that was your plan, we'd be halfway there by now. Spare me your toothless threats."

"Toothless threats," he repeated, low enough that she didn't think he meant her to hear. Luca glared. "For someone who came here to retrieve her betrothed, you have a funny way of showing that you want to marry me."

She laughed. She couldn't help it. The disgruntled look on his face was too much. "Luca ... Honey." And, yes, Cami injected a lethal dose of patronizing into her tone. "I have no intention of marrying you. I never did."

He blinked, shook his head, blinked again. "Clever little thing, aren't you?" he murmured.

His shock pleased her, but the new appreciation in his dark gaze pleased her more. For the first time since she'd arrived at the island, someone looked at her like they actually *saw* her. *Luca* looked at her like he actually saw her. He sat forward and braced his forearms on his knees. "What's the endgame?"

"Excuse me?"

"If you're not here intent on dragging me back to Thalania as your prize, you must have something else in mind."

She did, but while she may lust after this man, she couldn't trust him. His presence here only reinforced that truth. Instead, she deflected. "You would make a terrible prize. You're too big to haul around, too willing to glower at people you just met, and you're grumpy."

"I'm not grumpy."

She gave a theatrical sigh. "You're right. I shouldn't try to spare your feelings with kind words. You're not grumpy—you're an asshole."

He blinked. "Wow. Tell me how you really feel."

"My point is that I want a husband I don't have to win by traipsing through a jungle for seven days and avoiding people who want to deliver me bodily harm."

"When you put it like that ..." The distance seemed to shrink between them. Luca finally looked away. "You know, you don't have to play the prim prissy princess with me."

She didn't laugh this time, but the urge rose all the same. "Please, do tell me how I'm supposed to lay down all my defenses and depend on you to save me. Should you make a sling to carry me around so I don't stumble and turn my ankle?"

His lips twitched. "You get saucy when you're riled."

"And you get ridiculous when someone tells you no. I didn't ask for your help, and I'm doing just fine without you. Either this is all some ploy to ensure you win, though I can't imagine what you'd ask Death for that she wouldn't give you freely, or it's a trick of some other nature. I want nothing to do with it."

Luca pulled his pack forward and dug out an MRE. "Might as well eat while we argue."

She shouldn't. To follow even this small command, she set precedent of obedience—something Cami couldn't afford. On the other hand, not eating meant she'd be weak and worthless. In the humidity and heat, it was more important than ever to keep her strength up. She burned too many calories from hiking and sweating to not replenish them out of spite.

Slowly, reluctantly, Cami pulled out her own MRE. They set about getting the meals heating and sat back. She started to search for something to say, but then reality crashed down around her. For all intents and purposes, they were enemies. She couldn't trust him, and he certainly shouldn't trust her. Making small talk just to break the silence was a poor choice.

Apparently Luca hadn't gotten the memo. "Smart move you pulled back there."

She couldn't quite smother the curl of pride his words nurtured. "Oh?"

A tight smile pulled at his lips. They were really nice lips, sinfully curved and designed for wickedness. The shadow of stubble on his jaw only made that mouth all the more sensual. If she concentrated, she could almost imagine how it would feel to have him dragging his cheek up her inner thigh.

"Cami?"

She flushed, hoping the firelight hid her blush. "Sorry, I missed that."

"I can tell." There it was again, that tight smile that spoke of control just waiting to be shucked off. "Thinking virtuous thoughts?"

"Of course," she answered primly.

Luca chuckled, the sound raspy as if with disuse. "Right. Well, what you missed while you were over there thinking virtuous thoughts was my complimenting you on that take-down. I have a question, though."

She shouldn't poke him. It was like grabbing a tiger by the tail and hoping for the best. Cami couldn't help it. "I may or may not have an answer."

Another of those dry chuckles. "You knew I was coming and set a trap for me."

"That's not a question."

"*How* did you know I was coming?"

To tell or not to tell? She suspected he'd figure it out

eventually. Cami checked her MRE and found it fully heated. She took a cautious bite. *Not as bad as some of the ones I've eaten.* "You've been following me most of the afternoon. I didn't know it was you, of course, but I figured whoever it was would wait for night to attack. The rest is history."

"That didn't really answer my question. I might be a bit out of practice, but I know I didn't make any rookie mistakes that should have tipped you off. How did you know I was there?"

Answering that meant admitting just how deep her deception went. Admitting that showing up for the Wild Hunt wasn't simply a whim of a spoiled princess. That she'd planned and trained and sacrificed for this chance at freedom. Cami took another bite and chewed slowly. "It's enough to know I did." He frowned like he'd continue grilling her, so she turned the tables. "You said you're out of practice. You haven't participated in any of the Hunts since the tradition got started."

Just like that, his expression closed down. She hadn't even been aware that he'd started to let her in until he shut her out. "That's not a question."

She gave him the half smile that deserved. "Where did you learn this particular skillset?"

"A long time ago, it was the only thing that kept me and my siblings alive." He grimaced. "Well, that, and Amarante. She kept all of us alive."

Cami's breath stalled in her lungs. He was talking about what he'd gone through after he was taken. Questions bubbled up, but she clamped her mouth shut to keep them internal. Luca didn't know her. It wasn't right for her to demand answers when they were barely more than strangers, especially when the past obviously pained him.

The shadows from the firelight danced against the tall rock at his back, long and sinister.

She finally managed to swallow. "I'm glad you survived."

"Being out here ... It's so different, but it's fucking with me." He gave himself a shake and, just like that, the quiet pain disappeared. "So what's your plan?"

She let him change the subject, let the past sink back into darkness. Cami wanted to know what happened to Luca, how he was taken, what he'd survived. Those questions had haunted Yael for the entire time Cami had known the old woman.

The rest of the Nibley Family cared that one of their children had been taken and potentially hurt, but he'd been absent from Thalania more years than he lived there. He was a stranger and one potentially in line for their Head of Family. They were more than happy to let him stay in his little island paradise and leave them the hell alone. Even his parents had gone on to have more children, as if they could balance out the memory of the boy they'd lost.

Not his grandmother. Not Yael.

She'd never stopped searching for a way to bring him home, and when she'd eventually discovered that he was alive and well and occupying a little island in the Indian Ocean, she'd moved heaven and earth to try to bring him back into the fold. To bring him home. It hadn't worked, of course, and she'd ultimately decided that she wouldn't force the issue for fear of delivering her grandson more harm that he didn't deserve.

Now she just wanted answers.

Cami did too, if she was completely honest with herself.

She set aside her curiosity. Either there would be time to figure it out, or there wouldn't, but the Hunt had to come first. "I plan to win."

"That's not a plan. That's a wish."

Lord save her from this infuriating man. She lifted her chin. "I'm sorry, I must have missed the part where I asked for your help, your opinion, or your presence."

Luca gave her a lazy smile that had her stomach flipping over in slow motion. "You might not have asked for me, but you've got me. I'm not going anywhere."

9

Cami woke to the sound of groaning. Her hand went to her knife even before she opened her eyes. Seconds later she recognized the source. Luca. She sat up slowly, cautiously, but he lay where he'd put his sleeping bag on the other side of the fire. He'd managed to unzip it almost fully and, even in the low light of the embers, she could see his whole body was one tight line.

What to do?

In the end, it wasn't even a real argument. She climbed to her feet and moved to kneel next to him. Cami reached out and hesitated. He was obviously in the midst of a nightmare, and maybe touching him wasn't the best option. "Luca," she said softly. Firmly. "Luca, you're safe." It may be a little white lie in the strictest sense of the word, but she didn't care. "Luca, wake up. It's just a nightmare."

But he didn't open his eyes. Instead of calming, his breathing went even choppier. Damn it, she'd made it worse.

Cami considered and tossed her knife away. If she shook

him awake, she ran the risk that he wouldn't recognize her, that he'd see her as some kind of enemy and attack accordingly. She'd heard of soldiers having that reaction, and while she didn't think Luca had ever served officially, he obviously had demons stalking his dreams from the things he'd seen. Being on this island must have dredged them up.

She took a deep breath, braced herself, and put her hands gently on his shoulders. "Wake up, Luca."

The reaction was instantaneous. One second she was wondering if she'd have to shake him and the next she was on her back, one of Luca's hands around her throat.

He didn't choke her.

Even with his dark eyes unseeing and violence telegraphing from every line of his body, he didn't actually hurt her. Cami lay perfectly still, even though he had to feel her heart racing against his palm. "It's me, Luca. Cami. You're safe."

Slowly, so, so slowly, his gaze cleared, though he still looked positively haunted. "Cami."

"You're safe," she repeated.

He laughed hoarsely. "Not that. Never that." His gaze dropped to her mouth, and he released her enough to stroke her throat with his thumb. "Did I hurt you?"

"No." Was that her voice? She sounded as rough as if he *had* strangled her. Cami licked her lips. She couldn't help it. She wasn't sure she wanted to, no matter that playing with this man was the height of stupidity.

Luca shifted, settling more firmly between her thighs, letting the weight of his hips pin her. "You shouldn't have touched me while I was dreaming."

The fact he could lecture her while she felt his hard cock pressed against her was so typically Luca that she almost laughed. Instead Cami stopped waiting for him to decide what to do with this thing and hooked the back of his neck, pulling her upper body off the ground to kiss him.

He stayed perfectly still for the space of a breath, as if shocked that she'd gone there. Then he growled against her mouth and his hands were in her hair, cushioning her head against the ground as he ravished her with lips and tongue. He nipped her bottom lip, eating her gasp and sucking on the spot as if to soothe her.

Sensations rolled over her, his mouth on hers, his big body caging her even as he kept the majority of his weight off her, his cock insistently grinding against the seam of her pants. A little more pressure, a little more friction, and she just might come apart from this alone.

Luca kissed along her jawline and dragged his mouth over her throat. "This is a mistake."

"You keep saying that." She hooked one leg around his waist, trying to get a better angle. It was no use. There were too many clothes between them. Cami's breath sobbed out in frustration. "I need more."

He rolled off her. Before she had a chance to process the sudden absence, he took up a position next to her and urged her onto her side, her back to his chest. *Not again.* She tried to turn to face him, but he pushed her hair off her neck and pressed an open-mouthed kiss there. "Let me take care of you."

"You're not going to just lie there while I masturbate on whatever limb you deem acceptable this time?"

He cursed and his grip on her hip spasmed. "You've got a filthy mouth for a princess."

"I've got exactly the right kind of mouth for a sexually frustrated princess, you jerk."

"Can't have that." He slid one arm under her and pulled her closer to his body. With the other, he undid her button and zipper. Slowly. Achingly slowly. "I'm going to touch you now." It wasn't quite a question, but he didn't follow through on his declaration, his fingertips pressing lightly to her stomach just above the gaping band of her pants.

"Do you think this will work?"

He froze. "What are you talking about?"

She shouldn't have said anything, should have just allowed him to steer them. Last time it worked out so well, she could already feel pulses of anticipation surging through her body in a few key spots. But Cami had allowed herself to be swept along for the entirety of her life. "This." She rolled her hips, pressing her ass against his cock. "Flipping me over so you can't see my face. Taking up a position as if I could be anyone." She knew better. She wondered if he did.

His fingers flexed against her stomach. "This can't mean anything."

"Agreed."

He growled against the back of her neck. "You didn't even hesitate."

Oh yeah, this wasn't just someone feeling horny in the jungle. She pressed her lips together to keep from chasing that thought any further. Most of the time she wasn't even sure she liked Luca—she certainly *didn't* like how he kept treating her like she was spun glass. Though, in reality, Cami had no one to blame for that but herself. She was the one who'd manipulated his expectations. Apparently she'd triggered some protective instincts that he wanted to pretend he didn't have, and now he was going to punish her with ... orgasms.

Seemed logical enough.

"I'm sorry." She rolled her hips again. "Was I supposed to cry and beg?"

He gave the slightest flexing of his fingers, a blatant tell of how her words affected him. She might have smiled if she didn't need his touch so much.

Wait a minute.

Why was she waiting for *him* to decide when to make this move? That's not the person she was supposed to be right now. Cami shifted and covered his hand with hers. "Touch me or get out of my way."

There it was again. That growl that sent goosebumps across her skin in a wave. Luca set his teeth against her skin. "Wouldn't take much, would it? I already know how you like it."

She pressed down on the top of his hand, and he let her guide it into her pants and beneath her panties. She bit her lip as his calluses dragged over her sensitive skin and pressed his fingers to her clit. Lower, guiding a single finger inside. She couldn't keep her eyes open. There was nothing to see but the fire, anyway, so she didn't bother to try. "Is this a kink of yours, Luca?"

He crooked his finger when she said his name. "Is what a kink of mine?"

"Letting me use you as my own personal sex toy." She lifted her hips, trying to work him deeper. It was hot, so unbearably hot, to manipulate his hand into giving her pleasure, but she wanted more. She wanted him right there with her. She wanted him *participating*. "I never thought passiveness was your thing, but I can get down with that if—"

He set his teeth against the sensitive skin at the back of her neck. "You talk too much." Luca withdrew his hand and shoved her pants down to her knees and lower, until he could spread her thighs wide with his rough touch. Two fingers pressed into her, almost gentle despite how roughly he'd removed the barrier of her clothes. "I'm craving the feeling of you coming apart for me again."

That made two of them.

If she let him, he'd finish her like this, replace her clothes, pat her ass, and send her back to her sleeping bag. Cami understood that on an intrinsic level. She could take this pleasure and give nothing in return. She probably even *should* do that.

No. I want more.

She pushed his hand away and rolled to face him. His shock was the only reason she got his pants undone in quick order. Luca grabbed her wrist. "What are you doing?"

They were so close, she'd have to move back to see his face, and she refused to do that. Luca wanted a reason to stop this, to put her back into the clearly marked boundary he'd created for her. She carefully extracted his hand from her wrist and replaced it between her thighs. "Don't stop touching me."

"This is a mistake."

"Now *you're* talking too much." She reached into his pants and he didn't stop her as she grasped his cock. "Impressive," Cami breathed. She gave him a careful stroke and then a rough one, gauging his response.

Luca didn't make her guess. He resuming his slow finger fucking with one hand and used his free one to cover hers, showing her exactly the kind touch he liked. Cami caught on quickly, adjusting her pace and grip to match, and he let his hand fall away.

Her lips found his throat. She wasn't sure how it happened. She kissed him there, feeling his groan vibrate through his skin. Pleasure danced through her, Luca expertly playing her body even as she did the same for him.

She had to fight to concentrate, not to break her rhythm as he pressed the heel of his palm against her clit.

So close ...

Luca crooked his fingers inside her and she was lost. Cami's back bowed with the strength of her orgasm. She barely managed to keep her cry soft and quiet. Barely. Her grip on his cock faltered, but it didn't matter. Luca rolled her onto her back and shoved her shirt up to her neck, baring her stomach and breasts. He roughly fisted his cock stroking once, twice, a third time, and coming in great spurts across her stomach.

Cami lay there in a daze and Luca dropped next to her with a curse. That just happened. That had most definitely just happened.

She was in serious trouble.

Fucking Princess Camilla Fitzcharles was out of the question.

No matter that his cock was already getting hard again. No matter that she lay there mostly naked with his come marking her pale skin. No matter that he craved hearing that sexy little whimper she made when she came. If he started fucking her now, he wouldn't stop until dawn, and they both needed their sleep and their focus. *Should have thought about that before you fingered her ... again.*

Damn it, he was fucking up.

"Luca?" A thread of something unidentifiable in her voice.

He slowly withdrew, but he couldn't stop himself from pressing a soft kiss to the spot where her neck met her shoulder. "There's still a few hours left to dawn. Get some sleep."

Cami rolled away from him and to her knees. If he expected her to blush and stammer and fumble back into her clothes ...

Luca should have known better by now.

She stared at him for a long moment, her cheeks and chest flushed, her eyes heavy-lidded with pleasure. "If this place is bringing out your nightmares, you shouldn't be here."

Luca blinked. "What?"

"That's what was happening, wasn't it? Nightmares because this place reminds you of *that* place in some way." She shook her head and pulled off her shirt to clean up his mess. If he thought Cami's breasts were perfection in that little tease of a swimsuit, they were even better without anything shielding them. Small and perfect, with rosy nipples he had the sudden urge to taste.

"Luca, stop staring at my breasts."

He jerked his gaze her to face. "Sorry." She didn't look turned on, or even pissed. She looked ... worried.

Cami refastened her pants and tossed her ruined shirt toward her pack. "There's working through your issues and there's being an idiot. Would you like to know which category you fall into?"

He sat up, suddenly less concerned about her being half naked and more about the words she lobbed at him like grenades. "That's none of your fucking business."

"You made it my business when you *stalked* me here." Cami started to say something else, but abruptly shook her head. "You know what? This conversation isn't worth the energy it takes to have it. You made your choice. Bully for you. I'm going back to sleep." She marched to her pack and pulled out another shirt. "You're welcome, by the way."

He watched her settle back in, completely at a loss. Luca might not be interested in opening himself up for this near-stranger—for *anyone*—but she had woken him before his nightmare reached its inevitable conclusion. He flopped back down onto his sleeping back and stared up at the starry sky. Even in the warmth of the night, he couldn't shake the biting cold that followed him into waking. He shuddered.

No matter what Cami thought, she was wrong. Some things a person worked through and got over. Some things followed a person to their deathbed. Maybe beyond.

What happened in hell was the latter.

He didn't have to sleep again to be back in the nightmare. Some nights it was more real to him than the room he slept in and called his own. Those were the times when Luca took to stalking the passages between rooms in the casino, watching monitors and doing everything necessary to remind himself that he was no longer living on the knife's edge. He had a place of his own. A chosen family who didn't ask more from him than he was able to give. The kind of security only massive amounts of money could supply.

Tonight, that wasn't an option.

He made himself close his eyes. The only thing more unforgivable than having nightmares about what was done to him in that place was letting those feelings of fear and lack of control bleed over into his waking hours. He refused to allow it.

Instead he walked back through his nightmare. One step at a time.

The feeling of the splintered wooden handle of the knife pressed into his hand. The icy-cold packed dirt of the pit against his bare feet. The murmur of spectators in the private stands placing bets.

And the terrified blue eyes of the first boy he'd killed there.

The nightmares weren't always of the pit. Sometimes they were the organized hunt that left yet more children dead. The ones who weren't fast enough, weren't clever enough—the ones who were tired of living in that place.

It had a name. Camp Bueller.

For Luca, it was and would forever be hell.

Luca took one breath. And then another. Piece by piece, he walked through their escape, how Amarante had managed to get all four of them out alive despite it being the dead of winter, and how they'd kept each other alive in their desperate trek out of the forest surrounding that place.

But it wasn't Amarante's face that came to mind like it normally did when the past rode him hard. No, the features formed in his mind's eye were paler, wide blue eyes, cropped dark brown hair, pert little lips ...

Fuck.

Even as he tried to stop himself from using Cami as a grounding image, his body relaxed into it. The iron band around his lungs eased, and his head stopped throbbing. *Fuck*, he thought again. She wasn't supposed to mean anything to him. He wasn't certain she *did* mean anything to him. He wanted her safe, but looking deeper into that ... No. Luca couldn't do it.

Then you shouldn't be on this island, and you damn well shouldn't be touching her.

He knew that. He could ignore things he didn't like, but he didn't make a habit of lying to himself. He wanted Cami. He felt protective of her. He even admired her for surprising him. None of those things were uncomplicated on their own. Together?

It spelled a whole shit ton of trouble for Luca.

He blinked a few times into the near-darkness and let out the breath bottled up in his lungs. It didn't matter what he thought of her, because the plan had to stay the same. This whole thing was bigger than him, bigger than this hunt and this group of people.

Fifteen years, they'd waited for their revenge. First, because they were too young and nowhere near strong enough. Then later, because their fledgling business was too new to accomplish what they set out to do.

Fifteen years of building their own little empire in order to be strong enough to take on the demons of their shared past. It was finally time. He couldn't let a little thing like infatuation get in the way of justice.

Revenge.

Justice.

Two sides to the same coin.

The end result remained the same—they would cut the head off the snake that was the organization that stole them as children. They would kill those responsible and burn the remainder to the ground. They would salt the metaphorical ground behind them, ensuring the big players thought twice about trading in children.

Would it take the flesh trade out at the knees?

No. He wasn't naive to believe that.

But it would cut off part of it. And then ... They might not have talked about what came *after*, but he didn't think for a second that any of them would be satisfied. There were always monsters to fight, to drag down into the darkness and never let loose again. It might be thankless work, but it was important. Vital, even.

It all started with the Bookkeeper. He held the key to the organization. He had the names, the locations, and most importantly—the money.

Getting him onto the island was the only thing that mattered, even if it damned Luca's chances with Cami in the process.

He almost smiled. His chances with Cami? When the hell had he gone from wanting her to get the hell back to her safe little palace to flat out wanting her around? She was a princess in need of protection, and if he'd been good enough for her by birth when he was a child, he'd since become tainted beyond all recognition. Cami even understood that—it was why she really hadn't intended to marry him when she came to the island.

Luca set it aside. He needed to be focused and on his A game. Anything else was inexcusable. Slowly, oh so slowly, his body got the memo that they weren't in the middle of a fight, and relaxed muscle by muscle. He drifted into sleep sometime soon after.

Only to wake up to the sun grinding against his eyelids.

He blinked and sat up, already knowing what he'd find before he registered the empty spot where Cami's sleeping body had been only a few hours before. "*Fuck.*"

She'd gotten the drop on him.

Again.

10

Now that Cami knew Luca had the skillset to track her—that he was *there* on the island—she took great pains to cover her tracks. No matter how attracted she was to him, she couldn't trust him. Not during the Hunt. Maybe after ...

After didn't matter if she didn't win.

Nothing mattered if she didn't win. She'd come too far to be distracted now, even by Luca.

Especially by Luca.

She figured he'd expect her to either cut into the island or continue south. She went north instead. The route would take her dangerously close to one of the extraction points, but it was a risk she had to take. No one would expect her to skirt so near the very location she needed to avoid. Hopefully. The entire morning, she kept looking over her shoulder, half expecting Luca to appear, charging after her like a maddened bull. As the hours stretched through the morning and into the afternoon, she refused to acknowledge the sinking feeling in her stomach. It wasn't disappointment. It couldn't be.

By the time the sun started its slow descent toward the horizon, Cami made herself set aside thoughts of Luca. At some point she'd have to deal with him, especially if her plan to remove the other competitors played out like she hoped. Eventually there would be no one left but her and Luca and, no matter what he said about protecting her, she didn't think for a second he'd allow her to win.

No, her only option was to ensure her victory herself.

That meant she had to leave the relative safety of the beach. If there were any traps near the water, she hadn't come across them yet. Cami would never win in a fair right. She could shoot relatively well, but that wouldn't help her in a place where guns weren't allowed. Besides, she didn't really want to kill anyone if she had a choice. She could win without drawing blood.

She hoped.

Of her opponents, only one left was a woman and though she wasn't particularly large, Cami still didn't like the look of her. The assassin moved like the specialized security forces Yael had brought in at one point to teach Cami some of the finer bits of hand to hand combat. Those mercenaries had raised the small hair on the back of her neck. The other woman competitor did the same. She wouldn't underestimate Cami the same way the men would, and the usual tricks wouldn't work, either. It would require a different technique.

Worry about her later.

In a test of brute strength or brawling, every single one of the men would outmatch Cami. She could grapple a little, but her skills lent better to sneak attacks and ambushing than head-on combat. She could use that. She just had to be careful.

No two ways around it, though. She'd have to go deeper

into the cloying green to find the tools she needed to win this thing.

This is what I trained for.

She stopped and drank some water, thinking back to the moment when her whole life changed. The moment when Lady Nibley first acknowledged her. It was the summer after Cami turned eighteen. The old woman traveled to the palace to attend the wedding of Cami's middle brother, and she'd pulled Cami aside.

Those dark eyes had held knowledge Cami could only begin to guess at. *Your brother failed to bring my boy home.* She'd clasped Cami's shoulder with one of her gnarled hands. *Are you content here, girl? A nightingale in a cage, singing prettily. Off to marry someone—not my boy, of course, he's never coming home and an old woman has to make her peace with that. Some equally pretty noble who'll get pretty children from you. They'll never see the throne. Not with your two older brothers intent on breeding like rabbits.*

Cami pressed a hand to her chest, smiling now at the shock she'd felt back then. *What are you saying?*

You get tired of playing the princess, you come see me, girl. Could be you were destined for greater things. She'd shrugged. *Or could be that you're just as useless as everyone seems to think. Pretty and weak and in need of shelter.*

Cami had barely waited a month before she accepted Lady Nibley's invitation to spend the summer in her country estate. And so had begun her secondary education in a variety of things that a sheltered pretty princess wasn't supposed to know.

She gave herself a shake. She was finally here, finally doing the one thing Yael had asked of her in exchange for the invested years and resources. *Find answers.* Yael had made her peace with his not wanting to return to Thalania.

Now she just wanted answers. Answers to what happened to Luca all those years ago. Answers to who was responsible. Answers to what he intended to do with the rest of his life.

Once she delivered that information to Yael ...

She didn't really know what would be next. She would have her freedom in a way she had never experienced before. Not even Theo could argue that she wasn't able to take care of herself after she'd won the Wild Hunt. And with Death's favor in her pocket, he'd *have* to let her go.

Getting ahead of yourself.

First you have to win.

She wouldn't manage that while mooning about, thinking about things best left alone. Yael wasn't here, and if Cami missed her as if the old woman had actually been her grandmother, then that was a strange form of homesickness she needed to put aside. It wouldn't serve her now.

She took a slow breath and ducked into the trees. Searching the island wouldn't work, because she needed the traps more than she needed to find her opponents. *They* would find *her*. Cami simply had to be ready when they did.

It took her another two hours before she found the first trap, and by then the light had dimmed into something too close to night to risk moving farther. This one wasn't a cage like the last. It was an actual pit in the ground. She carefully shifted the clever mat—a heavy cloth with dirt and leaves and branches attached to it—away from the opening. The only reason she'd noted it in the first place was that it had the faintest outline showing in the long shadows of the setting sun. At any other time of day, she likely would have missed it.

Maybe she would have even walked right over it.

Cami pressed a hand to the smooth wall. Metal. There would be no chance at all of scaling it. She guessed it had to be at least ten feet deep, sheer walls a little too far apart to successfully leverage a person's body against to inch up. She studied the gap. It was a leap, but if someone chased her, if she was sprinting, she could make it. She just had to ensure she didn't jump too soon.

It took several minutes to get the mat back over the opening and another few to ensure it wasn't readily apparent that the pit existed. By then it was dark enough that she shuddered.

She couldn't risk a fire tonight. If she could guarantee that someone approaching would do it in the direction of the pit …

But no. It was too great of odds to attempt. Better to tuck herself up into one of the trees and wait for the light of morning. Cami sighed. She would kill for a shower and a soft bed, but five more nights lay between her and that particular goal.

Just five nights.

She could do this.

She shook her head and scaled a nearby tree, climbing until she couldn't be reached easily from the ground. She wedged herself in between two branches near the trunk. Two power bars were her only dinner, and then there was nothing left to do but think.

She hadn't wagered on her attraction to Luca. She definitely hadn't wagered on *his* attraction to *her*. No matter what his reason was for participating in the Hunt, Cami didn't doubt for a second that he wanted her.

Just like she didn't doubt for a second that he absolutely didn't *want* to want her.

Complicated did not begin to describe their situation.

Maybe it was just sex?

Maybe *she* was the only one complicating things. Surely

Luca didn't actually feel the protective urges he claimed, surely it was all part of Death's ultimate game.

Surely, surely, surely.

Cami couldn't be certain, though, and because she couldn't be certain, she couldn't quite make herself let it go. He was just so ... conflicted. Big and dangerous and so damn furious at her because of the desire he obviously felt. For all that, he'd touched her in a way that almost felt like caring, had prioritized her pleasure over his own not once, but twice. Cami had had lovers, albeit not many. Most of the eligible men in her country feared both her brother and his Consorts too much to touch her. It didn't matter that Theo had never pulled that misogynistic protective older brother bullshit. All he and her brother-in-law had to do was *look* at a guy talking to her and he scurried away. They weren't even glaring. And while her sister-in-law, their third, wasn't nearly as large or imposing, Cami had caught her casually threatening a particularly jerky ex of hers.

Somehow she didn't think Luca would be scared off by a look from her family. Or even a threat. He'd probably glare at them and then do whatever the hell he wanted. That was more in line with his snarly personality than any of the simpering power plays she was used to.

She smiled into the darkness. It didn't matter. All this was fantasy. The truth was that, no matter how many orgasms he doled out, she couldn't trust Luca. What was more, she couldn't trust herself to stay logical where he was concerned, not if she was already indulging in fantasies of how he'd deal with her brother. No, Cami had to avoid Luca at all costs.

Her very future depended on it.

LUCA SPENT A VERY frustrating day and night searching for the princess. He'd expected her to continue south down the beach, but before noon, he'd realized that wasn't her route. There was no evidence of her along the tree line, either. Nor to the north on the beach.

She'd successfully evaded him.

Hell if that didn't make him like her even more. It wasn't a convenient feeling. He had no space for liking her. Protecting her? Fuck yeah. Wanting her? Inconvenient, but not entirely unexpected. Liking her paved the way for the kind of complication that could sideline a plan fifteen years in the making.

The concern beating in time with his heart was only because her out on the island alone meant she was an innocent in danger. Not because it was *Cami*, specifically, in danger.

Liar.

He stopped short. Damn it, he knew better than to lie to himself. It served the same purpose of crippling himself physically. Worse in some ways, it created a blind spot that could be taken advantage of by someone enterprising. If he couldn't admit that Cami had somehow gotten beneath his skin, then he opened up a weak area for his enemies to strike.

She mattered.

He cared whether she made it through this Hunt unscathed. The thought of one of those pieces of shit hurting her ...

Luca clenched his hands. He would find her. He would keep her safe.

He would betray her, yes, but at least she would remain safe in the process. If she never forgave him, well, that was a small price to pay. He'd lived his entire life up until the last week with little knowledge of the Thalanian king's little sister, and he'd continue for the rest of his life just the same.

Liar.

This time, Luca shoved the snide internal voice aside. It served no purpose to worry about the future beyond the Hunt. Beyond tempting the Bookkeeper to the island, beyond doing whatever it took to get him to name his employers.

Beyond finally getting the justice they deserved.

What was his attraction to a tempting princess compared to that? Attraction came and went. The only thing consistent was his found family. They understood him. They knew what he needed to get through this life with his sanity intact. How could he bring another person into that, show them the demons that plagued him, and expect them to understand?

No, better to keep others at a distance.

Better to keep *Cami* at a distance.

Should have thought about that before you stuck your hand down her pants.

Luca was so busy being irritated over his lack of control, he almost missed the sound of a boot scraping against rock. He spun around just as one of the competitors—Vann, one of the Bookkeeper's men—brought his knife down in a vicious overhand strike. Luca got his arm up in time to deflect the blow, but the blade cut through his skin easily. Better his arm than his back, but that didn't stop the pain from radiating through him.

"Not so tough without the other three at your back, are you?" Vann's accent spoke of Eastern Europe, though not quite as far east as Russia. The Bookkeeper might have brought in champions from far-flung locations to prevent Ryu from searching out his identity through those connections, but at the end of the day it didn't matter. Only one could win.

Unfortunately for Vann, it wouldn't be him.

Luca didn't bother to respond. The other man wanted to edge him into anger, to drive him to make a mistake. He ducked under Vann's next strike and delivered a devastating punch to his stomach. *Strike, strike, strike.* One hit after another, a combination he moved through as easily as breathing.

Vann was made of tougher stuff than he'd anticipated, though. He didn't go down, though he wove on his feet, bleeding from the cut on his cheekbone. He adjusted his grip on his knife and grinned through bloody teeth. "Good. Not good enough." He went after Luca faster than he should have been able to after that last hit.

Luca scrambled back a step, cursing himself for being too cocky. When was the last time he had a real fight, one outside the ring?

Too long.

He dodged another swing and pulled his own knife. A fucking *knife fight.* And, worst of all in some ways, it felt like slipping into an old skin he hadn't quite outgrown. He instinctively bent his knees, the better to maneuver and counterstrike.

All the expensive suits and technology and power and, in the end, he was still that boy in the woods, so filled with rage that he was more animal than human.

Vann stabbed at him. Too slow this time. Luca grabbed his arm and jerked him closer.

Right into Luca's knife.

The other man's eyes went wide and he cursed. "Fucking fool."

"I'm not the one bleeding out from a gut wound." He

shoved Vann to the ground. "You have an hour, maybe two, before that ends you. Tap out." Every competitor came with the equivalent of a panic button. Pushing it meant aid—and instant disqualification. Luca shrugged at the stubborn look on the other man's face. "Or try to stay in the game and die a hundred yards down the beach. Your choice." He cleaned his knife and slid it back into the sheath.

Then Luca turned and walked away.

He barely made it three steps when Vann's laugh stopped him cold. "You think you can keep that girl safe?" He laughed again and had to clutch his stomach as the sound devolved into something pain-filled. "Dolph is already tracking her. He's going to rip her to pieces while you're here fucking with me." Another laugh, low and vicious. "There will be nothing left for you to clean up when he's done with her."

Fear spiked, cold and cloying. There was no way Vann could know that. *Luca* didn't even know where Cami was on the island right now. "You're just talking shit."

"Keep telling yourself that."

He turned without another word and resumed his path north. Let the man die or call for help. Either way, he was one less person to threaten Cami. *One of them still has to win.* So be it. But not Vann. And not Dolph. That only left one of the Bookkeeper's people. He'd have to be careful about eliminating targets going forward, but he wasn't saintly enough to let himself be taken out of the game to preserve Amarante's plan.

Especially now.

11

C ami had never been particularly patient. It was a skill her oldest brother excelled at. Playing chess with him was a lesson every single time, because she invariably did something impulsive, and within three moves, he'd achieved checkmate. Every. Single. Time.

She couldn't afford to be impulsive now.

She'd scouted the area around the pit, ensuring that there were no other traps to avoid, and plotting different courses that would bring her back to her destination. The temptation to simply keep heading inland until she found someone was almost too strong to deny, but she ignored it.

This was how she would win.

It was afternoon before her patience bore fruit. Footsteps sounded through the trees just north of her position. Cami held her breath from her spot in her tree, waiting until she caught sight of the man before she moved. He wasn't one of those attached to the large group of competitors, and he wasn't Liam. No, this one was the lone guy who hadn't bothered to talk to anyone as best as she could tell. She hadn't been able to get a good read on him back on the small island, but there was a desperation to his movements here. Whether that was because of the jungle itself or the Hunt, she had no idea.

In the end, it didn't matter.

Cami dropped to the ground as quietly as she could just to the south-west of him. She let herself make a pained whimpering sound and was rewarded when he froze. *At least he's capable. That makes this more believable.* She hurried in the direction of her trap, making so much noise through the trees that she had to stifle a wince.

"Princess." His low voice almost stopped her cold, but she was committed to this plan.

She cast a panicked look over her shoulder and picked up her pace. He cursed and did the same. "I'm not going to hurt you, princess, but I have to win this." Still with that low tone, and damn but he sounded almost regretful. Some of the competitors might be monsters, but she didn't think this one was.

Something akin to guilt spiraled through her, but she ignored it. The endgame was all that mattered. Cami slowed the tiniest bit until he was right on her heels, almost close enough to reach her.

And then she leapt over the pit.

They were moving too fast from him to course-correct, even if he'd realized what she was doing. She landed on the other side and took three large steps. He crashed through the thin mat and into the pit.

Cami dropped to the ground and pressed a hand to her racing heart. *Holy crap, it worked.* She'd hoped it would but … But it *had*. Her euphoria withered away in the wake of his curses.

Reluctantly, she crawled to the edge of the pit and looked down at him. Gone was the reluctance. He threw himself against the walls like a crazed person. "Goddamn it! Let me out!"

"I'm sorry." She wasn't. Not really. She'd only done the same thing he'd intended—whatever it took to win. "It's not personal."

"You don't fucking understand." He jumped, missing the top by a bare six inches. "I *need* this win! My sister needs me to win. *Goddamn you, let me out!*"

There was no use apologizing again. They all had their reasons for being there and if she felt bad that he wouldn't get the favor to help his sister or whatever his reasoning was, she couldn't let that guide her actions. "I'm sorry," she said again.

Cami rose and walked to where she'd stashed her bag. With his curses still ringing in her ears, she pressed her lips together to keep yet another apology inside and hurried away. He'd attract other competitors, if only to see what had happened to him. She didn't *think* any of them would help him out of that pit, but best if she wasn't here to find out.

She was so busy trying to put as much distance between her and his yelling that she forgot to check her surroundings. One moment she was striding purposefully through the trees, the next something closed around her ankle and yanked her feet out from beneath her. Her head hit the ground and then she was airborne, dangling several feet off the jungle floor. She'd lost her bag in the scuffle, and it landed several key inches below her fingertips.

Cami twisted, trying to get a better look at what held her. It seemed to be a simple snare, and she cursed herself for missing it in the first place. *Easy enough fix.* She took a breath and slipped her knife out of its sheath. At least she wouldn't have far to fall once she cut the snare.

It was still going to hurt.

She braced herself and bent in half, swiping up to cut the rope.

She never made contact. A hand closed around her wrist, neatly divesting her of her blade. She twisted away, well aware that he chose to release her. Spinning, spinning, until her motion finally slowed enough for her to get a good look at him.

Luca.

She should have known.

The arm of his gray shirt was stained with blood and he looked absolutely furious. *Luca, furious? Color me shocked.* He waved her knife at her, though she noticed he was careful to keep it well away from where her body swayed. "Who's in that pit back there?"

He was going to interrogate her? *Really?* She crossed her arms over her chest, and then felt silly for doing it upside down. "Cut me down."

"Answer the question."

"I don't know." She huffed. "Not Liam, not the woman, and not one of the group that seems to be working together. Will you let me down now?"

"Bellamy." He spoke the name in a contemplative kind of way. "Good." Luca crouched down until he was almost even with her face. "Promise me that you won't run again and I'll cut you down."

Like *that* was going to happen. "You can fuck right off with that blackmail."

"Language, princess."

The fact he was tsking her when every other word out of his mouth was "fuck" might have made her laugh if she wasn't so ready to scream. "Cut. Me. Down."

"Promise."

Oh, screw this. She bent in half and scrambled to grab

the rope around her ankle. If he wouldn't return her knife so she could cut herself down, she'd just figure out a way to untie herself.

Except her hands slips on the greased rope. "You have *got* to be kidding me."

"Honestly, do you think we'd set traps that are possible to get out of?"

Considering the quality of the cage and the steel walls of the pit, she should have known better, but Cami wasn't in the mood to be forgiving. She glared up at him. "Fine. You win. I won't run from you." *Until you're looking the other way and I'm sure I can escape.*

Luca chuckled. "If you're going to lie, you should be more convincing."

"Forgive me if I'm not in the mood to put a pretty face on your blackmail. Would you prefer a notary agreement or would a blood oath suffice?"

His chuckle rolled into an honest to god laugh. "You're kind of cute when you're pissed."

Okay, she wasn't going to run from him. She was going to kick his teeth in. "And considering the two women you call sisters, I would think you'd be smarter than to laugh at a woman furious with you."

That sobered him, though there was still something like merriment in his dark eyes. "I concede that point. At least give me a chance to talk before you make a run for it."

"You had your chance to talk. I listened. I am disinclined to play damsel to your knight in tarnished armor." She should be smart and at least make the appearance of giving him what he wanted, but Cami was too frustrated to bother. He'd see right through it no matter what she tried.

"We find ourselves at an impasse, then." He straightened

and looked around. "You know, his yelling is going to draw others."

"I'm aware," she gritted out.

"It would be a shame if they found you hanging here like a prize just waiting to be grabbed."

Oh, she was most definitely going to make him pay for this. "You're a crappy protector if you're just going to leave me for whoever comes by first. I suppose that answers my suspicions about how trustworthy you are—as in, you *aren't*."

His jaw went tight. "We'll continue this conversation later." Luca moved closer, dodging her kick easily and cut the cord attached to her ankle. The ground rushed up, but he caught her around the thighs before she could hit, and then lowered her to the ground.

She had every intention of running immediately, but the blood rushed from her head and spots danced across her vision. "I really don't like you very much right now."

"You weren't saying that last night."

He just had to go there, didn't he? She pressed her fingers to her temples. "Don't be an asshole just because I'm not tripping over my feet to let you help me."

Luca opened his mouth, seemed to reconsider, and shut it. "I *am* an asshole. Painting me in a different light is only going to disappoint you."

Cami closed her eyes and strove for patience. She couldn't tell if he was legitimately trying to be a decent guy and just failing miserably, or if he was ... She didn't even know what the other option was. If Luca wanted to use her to win the game, he could have done it the first night. If he wanted to use her to ensure the *right* person won ...

She'd just have to outmaneuver him.

Obviously that wasn't going to happen by fleeing,

because he kept finding her. *She'd* just have to use *him* until the competitors were down to a single number and then escape that way. Surely if she kept moving, she could stay ahead of him?

Cami wouldn't know until she tried.

She pasted a sweet smile on her face even though she still wanted to kick him in the shin. "I'll take that into consideration. Shall we get moving?"

LUCA DIDN'T TRUST this new amiable Cami, but the change served his purposes so he didn't question it. Yet. He glanced at the camera situated in the tree across from them, the perfect spot to capture this trap and anyone caught in it. They had to keep up appearances.

He grabbed Cami's arm and hauled her into the trees. There would be another camera ... Ah, there it was. "Keep your head down."

"I really, *really* don't like you right now."

"Trust me."

She snorted, which was no more than he deserved. He hadn't done shit to earn her trust, and the next few days wouldn't do anything to change that. Luca kept them moving at a fast march until they reached a spot where the cameras weren't positioned so closely together. Only then did he release her.

Cami immediately edged away from him. "You have a plan."

It wasn't quite a question, but he still treated it like one. "We're three competitors down. Bellamy, Brianna, and Vann. That only leaves Liam, Dolph, Edward, and Envy."

She blinked. "The other goon's name is Edward?"

"Yes. Weren't you paying attention during introductions?"

"I missed introductions, Luca. I'm the White Stag. We don't get to cozy up with the competitors."

That was right. He'd forgotten that the first dinner was more informal. The naming of the competitors was a ritual that happened right before they took off in pursuit, and Cami hadn't been there for that. "Sorry."

"Are you apologizing for forgetting that I wasn't in the room? Or for the fact that I'm being hunted right now as we speak?"

"For all of it."

Cami looked like she wanted to rip him a new one, but she sighed. "We should keep moving."

We.

He had no business looking into that word, but he liked the way it rolled off her lips. It wouldn't—couldn't—last, so he shoved it from his mind and moved closer. "We have to keep up appearances."

Understanding flashed through her blue eyes. "I suppose that would skew the bets if they thought I had inside help."

"Exactly." And it could spook the Bookkeeper. Luca took Cami's arm. "I have somewhere safe we can spend the night and plan—away from the cameras."

"Four days left." She glanced over her shoulder, where they could still hear Bellamy yelling. She flashed Luca a guilty look. "He sounded like he had a really good reason for being here."

"All the competitors have a good reason for being here. It's too dangerous a game to play unless they're desperate for the prize." *Or are being paid enough to secure it for someone else.*

She finally nodded. "I suppose you're right."

There was nothing else left to say. He towed her behind him, careful to keep his grip light and his pace even. Not that Cami had any difficulties keeping up. She moved through the jungle nearly as easily as he did, just as comfortable here as she'd been in that pink gown and heels.

Just as comfortable as she was in that tiny bikini.

Why shouldn't she be comfortable? She's a princess. She has a place in the world, power and protection in equal measures. She lives a charmed life. His thoughts held none of their previous irritation, though. Being a princess hadn't taught her how to trap an enemy, how to use the trees and surroundings in her favor. It hadn't taught her to set an ambush and follow it through. She'd learned that skillset elsewhere.

She'd *earned* that skillset.

Questions rose from deep inside him, a long-buried curiosity surging to the fore. He wanted to know how a pampered princess ended up on this path, what she thought to accomplish with a favor from Amarante, what she planned to do after the Hunt was over.

More damning, he wanted to know if she ever took off the masks she presented the world. He craved the knowledge of which Cami was the real one—the snarling feral thing in the jungle, the tempting siren on the beach, or the ice queen who'd walked through the doors of the casino? Maybe it was none of them. Or all of them. Luca didn't know, and it drove him to distraction.

They encountered no one through their forced hike to the destination he'd set, which was just as well. He had a feeling Cami would bolt the second he was distracted, and he couldn't hold her and fight to protect her at the same time. He needed to convince her that staying with him was her best bet, and the only way to do that was to have a conversation.

You've had conversations with this woman. Several. And none of them turn out like you plan.

Luca breathed a silent sigh of relief when he heard the crashing sound of the waterfall. Safe. They were almost safe. At least temporarily. As they walked through the line of close trees, he couldn't help but look back to catch the expression on Cami's face. She didn't disappoint.

Shock and pleasure.

Suspicion.

Luca didn't give her a chance to demand answers. He just led the way to the hidden ledge that ran behind the waterfall. It was almost invisible until a person was right on top of it, and in the years they'd run this hunt, no one had ever found the cavern behind it. Kenzie used it when she needed somewhere safe to rest, but she never visited it more than once during a Wild Hunt. Too easy for their competitors to cry foul if there wasn't regular images of her scrambling across their monitors. If she occasionally disappeared for a few hours at a time, no one thought too much of it. The island's camera network was exhaustive but not infallible.

They'd planned it that way.

He kept a hold of Cami's arm, ensuring she didn't fall. Again, he shouldn't have bothered. She was surefooted as she followed him behind the curtain of water and slipped past him to examine the cavern. If it could be called that. It was a natural space roughly ten by ten feet, with a mostly flat ground and a gap in the ceiling to let in natural light. The rock even broke through the worst of the heat, and the pool of the waterfall edged into this space several feet. Plenty of space for a quick bath.

If he wanted to keep from getting distracted, thinking about a naked Cami rising out of that pool of water was *not* the way to go.

He released her and moved as far into the cavern as he could. The minuscule distance did nothing to dampen his awareness of her, but at least he wasn't touching her. Luca shrugged out of his pack and let it drop to the ground. As much as he wasn't thrilled with the idea of fantasizing about her bathing, *he* was determined to scrub the sweat and dirt and *forest* from his skin. Fifteen years, and he hadn't been dirty like this in all that time.

It was as if his brain had waited until that very moment to register just how filthy he was.

Fuck.

He couldn't handle it.

He had to get clean.

Now.

Luca yanked his shirt over his head. Not enough. He had to get these clothes off. He dropped to the ground to muscle off his boots.

"What are you doing?"

He couldn't ignore her. Damn it, but it took more effort to speak than it should have. "I need to get clean," he ground out.

"Now? Are you serious?"

"Turn around if you don't want to see." He kicked off his socks and his hands went to the front of his pants. Luca forced himself to stop, forced himself to breathe past the panic. "Cami, I'm sorry, I just can't—"

"It's okay." Gone was her shock, her anger, replaced by calm. "Is there anything I can do?"

She knows.

It didn't matter if she understood completely or not. She'd read him well enough to figure out that something was wrong. He'd decide how he felt about that later. Right now, he had to get the rest of his clothes off and get into the goddamn water. Luca stripped in seconds and had enough restraint to slip into the water instead of leaping. The waterfall might hide them from anyone looking, but there was no reason to take stupid risks.

He ducked under the water, sinking as deep as he could, the full three meters to the floor of the pool. He caught the edge of a rock to keep himself in place and exhaled slowly, a tiny stream of bubbles escaping his mouth to join the roar of the waterfall overhead.

Slowly, painfully slowly, his panic abated and his mind cleared. He wasn't safe, but he wasn't in the same kind of danger he'd lived with for what had felt like time unknowable as a child. No he knew it was fewer than two years. Such a short time in an everyday life. When a person was in hell? It spanned an entire lifetime.

He waited until his lungs screamed for air and he couldn't stand it any longer before pushing off the bottom and swimming to the surface. Cami sat a foot back from the edge, a worried expression on her face. It disappeared as soon as his head cleared the water, but he saw it nonetheless.

She was worried about me.

He scrubbed a hand over his face and winced. "Can you bring my pack over?"

"Soap?" She held up a white bar that he hadn't noticed she held. "It's unscented." Cami passed it over and Luca decided not to comment on her anticipating his needs. Of course she knew what he needed. When he'd just stripped like a madman, barely capable of speech and submerged himself until he couldn't stand holding his breath any longer ... It didn't take a genius to figure out what had bothered him.

He still appreciated it.

"Thanks." He found a small ledge underwater to stand on and got to work cleaning the feeling of filth from his skin. It wasn't completely imagined—several days in the heat and humidity was more than enough to make them both a little ripe—but it wasn't anywhere near as bad as his mind tried to convince him. Memory overlaid reality, the dried sweat turning into several days' worth of mud and worse.

"Do you want to talk about it?"

He started to shake his head, but she deserved some kind of explanation. "When I was a kid, there was a period of time when I didn't have access to ... Well, to anything resembling cleanliness. It doesn't normally bother me, but when it gets triggered, I can't think until I get clean." Luca braced himself for questions, for demands for more information.

But Cami just nodded. "Being part of the Hunt must be hard for you."

He soaped up his hands and scrubbed harder across his face. When he ducked under the water and came up again, he could finally breathe. "Kenzie is usually the one out here, and she doesn't have the same hang up." He shuddered before he could stop himself. "My sister is batshit crazy."

"I'm sure she has her own issues."

Kenzie had more masks than Cami seemed to, and even though she gave every appearance of casual contact and allowing people close ... She didn't. She kept them at just as much of a distance as Amarante did. She was just less obvious about it, all smiles and flirting and swagger until people didn't realize they knew next to nothing about her, that she'd never actually let them in. "We all do."

12

Cami kept every trace of sympathy off her face. Luca wouldn't recognize it as such. He'd think she pitied him, and he'd hate her for it. She just sat at the edge of the pool and tried to reconcile her vision of this powerful man with the reality of this deep wound he carried.

No matter what he thought, she wasn't a fool. She knew he'd gone through something unspeakable. People did not steal children for any angelic reason. It had been years before Yael's people found him, and by then he'd been nearly an adult and evaded all attempts to bring him home.

It still was something entirely different to see evidence of it on his body.

Scars crisscrossed his torso, his arms, and what little she'd seen of his legs before he'd slipped into the water. Long silver ones from blades, puckered ones that looked like puncture wounds, and several spots had the glossy smooth skin resulting from healed burns.

He looked like he'd been tortured.

Because he was. Whether it was in the most literal sense or through his experiences, he was tortured.

She met his dark gaze, her breath stilling at how haunted he'd become. "Is there anything I can do?" The question slipped free before she could think better of it. She wanted to smack herself. Was there anything she could do? How about not acting as if she knew a thing about what he'd gone through?

"The skeletons in my closet haven't been put to rest … yet. That's the only thing that can help." He gave a wan smile. "Though I appreciate the offer."

Meaning that the skeletons would be put to rest at some point. She sat back on her heels, understanding settling over her, the knowledge heavy enough she swore she could actually feel it. "That's what this island is, isn't it? A carefully designed trap for the ones who hurt you." No wonder no one from Thalania had been able to pull him out of this place. His motives went beyond money, beyond power.

He wanted justice.

Luca set the soap aside, disappeared under the water for a long moment, and then propped his arms on the ledge next to her. "I'm no saint. We've caught a shit ton of people in our nets, and not for altruistic reasons, either. Power is the only god we worship."

He could say that, but it didn't change the truth. She would wager every person they *trapped* led to their ultimate purpose. Power enough to go after those who hurt them.

Except …

She shook her head. "Yael searched for them. *Theo* searched for them after he took the throne, and his father did before him. No one found any evidence of the people who took you, who kept you. Even when they found you, they never found where you'd been held or any hint of who was responsible."

Luca shrugged. "They were careful. More than careful. Code names and masks and a secret location in northern British Columbia, far out from anything resembling civilization. Even we don't know their true identities and we were the ones trapped in that place."

Not being able to put a name and history to the person victimizing him and the others must have been ... She had to look away. She couldn't control what he'd see in her eyes. "What happens once you find them?"

Luca let loose a hoarse laugh. "You don't have any doubt that we will."

"Obviously." She finally had herself put back together again enough to face him again. "If I didn't know how carefully you four have cultivated your reputation, I would think you're fishing for a compliment."

He studied her, tiny rivulets of water tracing the lines of his face. "What are you really doing here, Cami?" She opened her mouth, but he spoke before she could figure out whether to offer him a lie or something resembling the truth. "We both know you're not here to use the favor to haul me back to Thalania. And you've admitted that the betrothal is bullshit."

"Did I?" She did—*couldn't*—trust him. If she put herself out there and he used it against her ...

He would use it against her.

Luca's loyalties lay with the other Horsemen. It lay with the Island of Ys. Even if by some strange turn of events, he felt loyalty to Thalania, that *still* wouldn't put him in Cami's corner. "It's private," she said stiffly.

"Keep your secrets, then." Only the slightest tensing in his shoulders betrayed that her refusal affected him. If he hadn't been naked, she never would have seen the small response.

He was naked.

Cami blinked, awareness rolling over her in a wave she didn't even try to resist. "Luca." Her breathy tone gave her away.

"Yeah?" He didn't move, just maintained his position, his eyes darkening even further as he took her in. "You looking to distract me because I'm dancing too close to the truth?"

No. Yes. Maybe. She licked her lips, all too aware of the way he tracked the movement. "I don't know."

"What *do* you know?"

For a man who almost certainly would have tossed her over his shoulder and bodily carried her to a helicopter that would transfer her off the island, her protesting all the while, he was almost cautious when it came to the attraction between them.

She shouldn't give in to her desire. It would cloud her mind. She wasn't cold enough to have sex with him without it changing things. They'd barely fooled around, and it had caused her to be unforgivably weak when it came to this man. If he was anyone else, she would have found a trap to trip around him and moved on to the next competitor threatening her win.

And yet ...

And yet.

What was the point of all her sacrifice and all her training if she was just going to continue denying herself the things she wanted more than she wanted her next breath?

Mistake or not, it was *hers* to make.

Cami unlaced her boots and pulled them off, quickly followed by her socks. She pushed to her feet, her hands suddenly clumsy, and pulled her shirt over her head. Pants, bra, panties. They all followed in quick succession, until she stood before him naked.

The temptation rose to jump into the water and avoid his slow perusal, but she planted her feet and met his gaze. Once they crossed this line, there was no going back. More importantly, it couldn't change anything for either of them. Luca still had his goals, and she knew beyond a shadow of a doubt that they were in direct opposition to hers.

Tomorrow it would matter.

Tomorrow she'd find a way to slip away from him and this time she'd make it stick.

But it wasn't tomorrow yet.

She took Luca's hand and let him guide her into the pool. The water was colder than she expected, but all the more welcome for it. Cami went under, and even in the darkness she couldn't shake the awareness of his presence. Almost close enough to touch. She surfaced and reached for the bar of soap.

"Let me."

She blinked, treading water. "I ... okay." She probably should have put up a fight, but she was so goddamn tired of fighting. Especially when this was something she wanted so desperately.

Cami let him pull her to the ledge where he stood. He lathered up the soap with his big hands and then they were in her hair. Luca weighed her hair as if it were made of gold and then carefully went to work soaping up her scalp, his fingers finding the tension spots where a headache threatened and massaging.

She moaned. She couldn't help it.

Several long minutes later, he moved down her neck and over her shoulders. "Up," he murmured, and she rose out of the water enough to allow him access to her breasts and back. He took equal time with both, his thumbs dragging over the lines of her back and then around and up her stomach to cup her breasts. The move brought his chest against her back and she shivered at the feeling of his cock pressing against her ass. "Luca."

"Not yet." He lifted her fully out of the water and soaped the rest of her body. His dark eyes traced the path his hands took, his brows furrowed in concentration. As if this was the main event, rather than the prequel to better things.

Finally, she couldn't take it any longer. Cami nudged him back with her foot on his chest and slid into the water. She submerged fully, running her fingers through her hair, but this time the cool temperature did nothing to dampen her need. She surfaced and he met her there, hauling her into his arms.

Her legs went around his waist in a move as natural as breathing, and he took her mouth, displaying none of the hesitation he had last time they kissed. Why should he? She was his, at least for the moment. He kept an arm between her and the rock wall, cushioning her back, and used the other to tangle in her wet hair, angling her head back for better access.

As if she would deny him anything in this moment.

Cami ran her hands up his chest and back down, loving the way his muscles flexed against her fingertips. She wanted to take her time, to give him the same treatment he'd lavished on her, but the desire in her blood was too strong to ignore. "Luca, I need you."

L*UCA, I need you.*

Had he ever heard those words before? Not like this,

desperate and full of desire. Luca pressed his forehead to hers, breathing harshly. It wouldn't take much in their current position. A shift of angle, a thrust of his hips. He'd be inside her with no more waiting.

It wasn't enough.

He lifted her out of the water and set her on the edge. "Not yet."

"Please—"

He gripped her thighs and pushed them wide, forcing her to prop her hands behind her in order to steady herself. "Not yet. Not until I've tasted you."

"I need you inside me," she whispered, but her hands went to tangle in his hair, nudging him between her spread thighs.

He kissed just above her knee and then dragged his cheek along her skin, loving the way she shivered in response. "*I* need to have you coming on my face."

Her hands spasmed in his hair. "That's a compelling argument."

"Mmm." He parted her with his thumbs, exploring her pussy with both sight and touch. He'd give an inordinate amount of money for some good lighting right now so he could see her in perfect detail, but the intimacy of the dim cave somehow made this perfect. He exhaled against her clit.

Cami tugged on his hair. "Don't tease me, Luca. I don't think I can survive it."

He moved back, enjoying the tiny sparks of pain from her grip, and kissed her other thigh. "Tell me what you want."

She spread her thighs wider, only her hold on him keeping her from falling. And fuck if he didn't like that. An offering without reservations, without conditions. Just this woman and her need for him. Cami's breath hitched. "I need your mouth on my pussy. Suck my clit. Fuck me with your tongue. Make me come on your face."

His cock went so hard he had to close his eyes for a moment to prevent himself from coming on the spot. Holy fuck, she was the sexiest woman he'd ever had the privilege of touching.

"Dirty girl," he murmured. "I fucking love it." Luca dragged his tongue over her pussy, exploring her with his tongue the same way he had with his fingers. It took everything he had not to fall on her like a mad beast, but less than thirty seconds in, Cami was writhing against him, pulling him closer yet.

"There. Right there. Keep doing that. Oh god, don't you dare stop."

Luca had half a mind to tease her, but that plan dissipated in the face of her need. He circled her clit in exactly the way she demanded, loving the way she slapped a hand over her mouth to muffle her escalating cries. Her thighs clamped around his head as she came. She held nothing back.

His princess orgasmed like a fucking porn star.

Luca didn't give her a chance to recover. He leveraged her down onto her back and wedged her thighs wide again. She whimpered. "Too much."

"Shhh. I've got you." He left her clit alone for now, but Luca and control were no longer on speaking terms. Her taste drove him mad and he licked and sucked and fucked her with his tongue until her hands were back in his hair and she rode his mouth like a wild thing.

A minute. Five. Twenty. Time lost meaning until she orgasmed again, her legs falling limply to the floor. Cami gave an almost hysterical laugh. "Holy shit."

He hauled himself out of the water and pressed a quick kiss to her mouth. "Don't move."

"As if I could."

It took a few minutes to get their sleeping bags laid out, and by then his skin had mostly dried. He bent down and scooped Cami up, ignoring her half-hearted protest. "If you try to walk right now, you're going to fall flat on your face."

"Arrogant."

"Accurate." He laid her down on the sleeping bag and hesitated.

Cami reached overhead and dug through her pack, coming up with a pair of condoms. When he raised his brows, she shrugged. "Don't look at me. They weren't in my pack when I got on the boat with War."

He didn't know if he should throttle his sister or thank her. Considering that Cami lay naked before him, Luca leaned toward the latter option. "My sister likes to meddle."

"I'll be sure to send her a gift basket." She ripped open the condom and sat up to roll it over his cock. "No more teasing. I need you inside me, and I need it now."

"What the lady wants, the lady gets." He kissed her, bearing them down to the ground and used his free hand to guide his cock into her. Slowly. Fuck, he needed to go slowly. Luca fought the urge to drive into her, the need only made stronger by the way she writhed against him and clutched his hips. "I'm going to hurt you."

"Don't care." She hooked one leg around his waist and arched up, sinking him another few inches into her. "More."

"Cami, fuck, just give me a second."

She released his hips to plant her hands on either side of his face, forcing him to meet those big blue eyes. "You won't break me, and you won't hurt me. Stop worrying about doing the right thing and *fuck me*, Luca. I can take it. I promise I can take it."

Another thing he couldn't deny her. Luca pushed the rest of the way into her, sheathing himself to the hilt. He half expected Cami to tense up, but she went molten in his arms. "More."

"Greedy girl."

"Yes."

Luca leveraged himself up, wedging his hands under her ass and lifting her hips with him. "Legs on my shoulders." He barely waited for Cami's rush to obey before he gripped her hips and started fucking her in earnest.

Her breasts bounced with each stroke, and hell if it wasn't a thousand times sexier than he'd imagined. She made everything better, hooking her ankles at the back of his neck and rising to meet him every time he plunged into her, her fingers digging into his thighs, her blue, blue eyes so fucking honest he could barely stand to meet them.

Oh yeah, his princess was loving every second of this.

"Touch yourself. I want to feel you coming around my cock."

She released one of his thighs and snaked her hand down her stomach to circle her clit. Brazen, sexy woman. Luca clenched his jaw, fighting against the orgasm he could feel drawing his balls up. Not yet. Soon, but not yet.

Cami's back bowed and he lunged down to take her mouth, eating her cry as she came. The new position sank him impossibly deep inside her, and he couldn't hold off any longer. Luca came hard enough to see stars. The world shifted on its axis and as he tried to relearn how to breathe, he couldn't shake the feeling that he'd shifted right along with it.

He carefully disentangled her legs and moved away long

enough to dispose of the condom in the bag at the bottom of his pack for trash. Luca laid down beside her, and Cami immediately rolled to tuck herself under his arm. "I thought there was no way it could live up to the fantasies and yet here we are."

He found himself grinning down at her. "Long time until dawn."

Cami frowned against his chest. "And only one condom."

"Guess we'll have to get creative."

She lifted her head and gave him a Cheshire Cat grin. "You know, there's one fantasy we haven't played out yet."

"Only one?"

"Give me some credit. I've only known you a handful of days, but I have an overactive imagination and a healthy sex drive." She trailed a single finger down the center of his chest to his stomach. "Let's try this again. I want to suck your dick, Luca." She arched up and nipped his earlobe. "Do you want to know how many times I touched myself to that fantasy?"

Fuck, this woman might actually kill him. "Is that a trick question?"

"Nope." She moved to straddle him, her grin soothing something in his chest that had been jagged so long, he barely noticed it until Cami's presence sanded it down to smoothness. "The answer is seven."

"Fuck."

"Mmm. Yeah, I had a lot of time on my hands." She laughed softly. "How far did you get after I came all over your hand on the beach?"

He could give her nothing but honesty. "I ducked into the first storage closet I got to inside the casino."

"Thought so." She took his hands and pressed them to

her breasts, sliding his palms down her body and back up again. "I'm too pent up. I need you again."

God, she was perfect. Completely and utterly perfect.

"Good. I'm nowhere near done with you yet." Luca gripped her hips and moved her up his body to straddle his face.

13

Cami woke up to Luca's fingers trailing along her spine. She smiled against her sleeping bag. "What time is it?" In the dark hours of the night, they'd brought each other to orgasm again and again, all lust and desperation and need. Every time, she swore she'd stay awake and leave, but somehow it never happened. She'd close her eyes for a moment and be woken the next with Luca kissing the back of her neck, or stroking a hand over her hip, easing her into wakefulness before he eased his fingers or tongue into her.

"It's time to go."

Her eyes flew open. "What?" Cami rolled away from his touch, the cold of the cavern rock floor stealing her breath. She welcomed the rush of clarity it brought. Above them, the natural skylight showed a clear blue. Not only was it morning, but the sun had fully risen. "How?"

"Morning usually follows night." He wore only his pants, and she pressed her lips together at the sight of Luca looking so deliciously relaxed.

It was a lie.

A second glance had her noting the tension in his shoulders and the tightness in his jaw. He might have affected a relaxed pose, but the man who'd seduced her last night was slipping away as she watched. He tapped her pack. "Or do you mean how did you manage to fall asleep instead of sneaking out?"

Shock slapped her in the face. She recovered, but not quickly enough. "I—"

"If your next words are going to be a lie, don't waste them."

Steel bled into her spine, straightening her shoulders and back. Cami lifted her chin. "You would have planned the same thing in my position."

"Undoubtedly." His gaze flicked over her body, molten hot and just as angry. "Why are you here, Cami? The truth."

Apparently the escape they'd offered each other had passed with the night. She tried not to mourn its loss. This had to happen. They didn't trust each other, and *that* wasn't going to change as long as they were on this island.

It might not change even after the Hunt was over.

She couldn't stay on the Island of Ys, and Luca had made it abundantly clear that he would never leave in any permanent way.

Permanent? Really, Cami? You know better. You're not some naive teenager who thinks that sex means anything other than a mutually satisfying experience.

Cami stalked over to yank her pack out of Luca's hands. He held on just long enough to let her know he'd *allowed* her to take it, and she wanted to scream in his face for ruining everything. Or at least ruining things before she had a chance to. Instead, she pulled out a set of clean clothes, and put entirely too much focus in donning them.

"Answer the question."

Fat chance of that. "I'm here for the same reason that everyone else is—to compete in the Wild Hunt and win." She dropped to the ground and grabbed her boots. Why had she thought this was a good idea? Oh, right, she *hadn't* thought it was a good idea.

She'd just done it anyways.

While her body still ached deliciously from what they'd done through the night, she couldn't quite dredge up the appropriate amount of regret. He still looked at her like he wasn't sure whether he wanted to lob her into the pool of water or take her against the wall, despite them already using the second condom. She knew which option had her vote, and that was enough to get her moving. Cami stood and snatched up her pack. "I've got to go."

"*We've* got to go." Luca shook his head. "But we need to have this conversation first. Tell me the truth, Cami. Why are you competing?"

Her chances of getting out of here without answering that question dwindled away to nothing. She could bolt, but he'd follow and, unless she was willing to try and hurt him, they'd just be having this same conversation in a few hours. Cami clenched her backpack to her chest. "Fine. You want to know the truth? I grew up in a glass box of a life. Yes, I've known loss, but ultimately I was surrounded by love and treated as breakable and something to be protected." Theo, more than anyone else, had stepped in after their father's death and taken it upon himself to fill father and brother *and* monarch roles in her life. He did it for love, because he had seen horrible things in this world and he wanted to spare Cami the pain of them.

It didn't change the fact that he'd been a big reason she moved through the palace, constantly feeling as if she were gasping for air. There was never enough. Not in the palace. Not even in the entire country. "There are only so many paths a princess can take. I can't have a real job. I can't have a normal life. I can't travel without a contingent of security shadowing my steps."

She sighed and tried to let go of her anger and frustration. In the end, it wasn't Luca's fault. It wasn't *anyone's* fault. "When I was eighteen, Yael Nibley saw that I was drowning and offered me a life preserver. She wanted answers about what happened to her lost grandson—*you*—and I wanted to be free to live something resembling a normal life. Thalania couldn't give either of us what we needed."

"She knew what happened to me." Luca's features might as well have been carved from stone. "Thalania has sent three delegations here to try to pry me away from the island. Not including you."

Cami shrugged. "They left without answers. She knew you were here, knew you were alive, but she had no other information, no matter how deeply her resources dug."

"So she ... what? Sent you as a sacrifice? She didn't honestly think you were going to win the Wild Hunt."

He was so damn sure of that, she wanted to throw something. "I've been doing just fine without your help. I would have been doing better if I wasn't the White Stag."

"Maybe." Now it was his turn to shrug. "This is all fascinating, but you haven't answered my question."

Cami closed her eyes for half a second and sighed. "I would think it's obvious, Luca. I want to be free."

"You don't need to win the Hunt to be free."

She finally let her bag drop back to the ground. "You don't understand."

"You're a princess. You probably have your own fat bank

account and private residence and a whole lot of shit normal people don't have. You have money and resources. You don't need a favor from Amarante."

He definitely didn't understand. She ran her hand through her hair. "Everything I have is connected to Thalania. Everything. Theo might never hurt me on purpose, but he fully expects me to fulfill the role set out for me. We're the royal family and we have a responsibility to the people." He'd said as much to her just a few months ago when she'd gone back to the palace for the birth of her most recent niece. She rubbed her hand across her chest at the memory.

"You'll never sit on the throne. Both your brothers seem like they're intent on breeding small armies of children, and every one moves you a spot further from being queen."

"Correct, but I'm still expected to fall in line. To pick some cause to champion that's not too controversial, and spend most of my time doing that until I finally agree to marry someone suitable."

"*Suitable* meaning ..."

"Either a noble from one of Thalania's Families or someone of equal rank in one of our allying countries. After that, there will be more than one child, but no more than four. I will have to show up to every event, looking above reproach, and do my part to ensure Thalania's power structure remains unharmed." Theo had never told her *that*, of course. Any of it. He wasn't cruel, especially with Cami, and if she came to him saying that she had fallen in love with a person who didn't have the prerequisite qualifiers, Theo wouldn't stand in her way.

But there was still the gilded cage her station represented.

"What are you saying?" Luca looked at her like he'd

never seen her before. "You don't want to be a princess anymore?"

"I'll always be a princess, Luca. No one—not even Amarante—can change that. I simply want my freedom."

He huffed out a low. "There's nothing simple about that."

"I'm aware. Hence the Hunt." She motioned at the waterfall, the cavern, them. For years, it felt like she'd been at the starting gate, bouncing in frustration and waiting for the signal to run. Now that she was actually in the race ... She didn't know what to think. Luca no doubt thought her quest for freedom was foolish—Yael had told her as much countless times over the years—but that was all Cami wanted. "It's the only way."

"Cami ..."

A shadow flickered over the natural skylight above them. That was all the warning Cami got before a woman dropped into the cavern. *The assassin*. She wore a dappled black and green catsuit that molded to her curvy body and had to make her damn near invisible in the trees. Cami barely had a chance to take a step back when the woman launched herself at Luca. The impact sounded meaty and painful as they hit the ground.

Cami cried out, but it was too late.

Their struggle sent them rolling across the ground.

Right into the pool of water.

EVERY INSTINCT LUCA had demanded he fight to the surface for another breath, but he shoved the impulse away. Instead, he clasped Envy around the hips, ignoring her striking him, and pulled her deeper. The pool wasn't *that* deep, but it would still serve its purpose. He pinned to them to floor as best he could. How long had they been under? Less than a minute, but the fight hadn't allowed either of them to pull in a full, deep breath.

Luca could outlast her. He had to.

She drew her knife.

The fact she hadn't until that point spoke more of her confidence than anything else. Or maybe she hadn't wanted to risk killing Cami in the struggle. It didn't matter.

He caught the faint glint off the blade before it slid into his shoulder. *Fuck, that hurts.* He didn't shrink from it, though. To pull away was to give her another chance to stab him. Instead, he leaned in, forcing her back until she knocked against the floor of the pool again.

Her breath escaped in a stream of bubbles. If he let her up now ...

But no, he couldn't risk it. Better to incapacitate her now and trigger her beacon than to leave her behind to keep hunting them. This woman—this assassin—was arguably one of the most dangerous people on the island, and removing her from the competition was just as important as ensuring the right person won.

Especially now that she'd found them.

Another stream of bubbles. She fought to get to the knife out of his shoulder, but her hands found no purchase. If they'd been on land, she might have stood a chance. Luca was good, but Envy was better. He had no doubt of that.

In the water, though?

She went limp, all fight disappearing in the space of a heartbeat. He should keep her down here longer, to make sure she wasn't faking, but Luca didn't want to *kill* her. He just needed her gone.

He pushed off the bottom of the pool and took them to

the surface. Cami crouched on the ledge, her blue eyes large with worry. Luca grabbed the edge and hefted Envy up. "CPR."

"Okay." Cami caught her under the armpits and awkwardly pulled Envy from the water. She lay her on her back and started CPR.

It took Luca two tries to pull himself back into the cavern. The knife might have missed anything too vital, but it still hurt like a bitch and affected the strength in his left arm. Damn it, he had to wrap up this Hunt sooner, rather than later. Taking on the remaining competitors would be tough, and that was if he operated at full strength. To do it while being cut up?

No use thinking about that.

"I think I just cracked her ribs," Cami murmured. She leaned down and breathed into Envy's mouth.

The woman seized and then water spilled from her lips. Cami immediately turned her onto her side as she coughed up water. Envy moved, but he moved faster. He grabbed her wrist and pinned it to the ground. "Tap out or next time I take you under, you die."

Her dark eyes burned with hate. "You're making a mistake, Famine."

"Wouldn't be my first," he answered easily. "You knew the rules when you signed up. You're leaving the Hunt either way, in a body bag or on a boat back to the casino to have a doctor look at those ribs that Cami just cracked. Decide."

Envy reached up with a shaking hand and pressed the button on the necklace hanging around her neck, holding it long enough to register her fingerprint. "You got lucky."

"Without a doubt." He glanced at Cami. "Time to go."

She nodded and wordlessly handed over his pack. He

stood and glanced at Envy. "You're welcome to stay here, but your best bet is to make your way to the coast."

"Fuck off," she hissed.

He nodded and motioned for Cami to precede him around the waterfall. He waited until her shadow on the water disappeared before he looked back at Envy. "This was a fair fight, and you know it. Don't think to come looking for revenge—or sending one of your sisters to try for it." The last thing he needed was to have the Virtuous Sins on his ass.

She looked at him for a long moment and struggled to sit up. "If I disagree?"

"Then it would be safer to kill you and be done with it. It's common knowledge that not all the competitors make it out of the Hunt alive. A risk we all took when we signed up."

Envy gave a tight smile, though her dark eyes were still furious. "Then you have nothing to worry about, Famine." It wasn't even in the same realm as a promise, but it would have to be good enough. He gave a short nod and followed Cami's path out of the cavern.

He half expected her not to be there when he emerged into the sunlight.

But Cami stood there with arms crossed, her expression worried. "You didn't kill her, did you?"

Luca stopped short. "You think I sent you out so I could off her without an audience?"

A shrug. "Even with her beacon triggered, she's still a threat."

He studied her, trying to figure out which way she landed on this. "Would *you* have killed her?"

"Not in cold blood," came the prompt reply. "In self-defense ... I don't know. I've never killed a person before."

Of course she hadn't. Even with the training she

possessed, normal people didn't practice watching the light fade from another's eyes. Most people never experienced it, went out of their way to *avoid* experiencing it. Luca cleared his throat. "She's alive. Furious and probably planning my death, but alive."

"Oh. Okay." Cami pressed her lips together. "Should you change before we get moving?"

Just like that. She didn't question him further, didn't demand an explanation or his reasoning. She just … moved on. "Yeah, give me a minute." He moved a little farther into the trees and changed quickly out of his wet pants and into his spare clothes. They were the last clean thing he'd brought onto this island, so short of washing his shit, he was out of luck for the next couple days. Luca tried not to let that knowledge bother him, tried not to curse himself and Amarante and Kenzie and even Ryu for his being in this situation to begin with.

The wet heat pressing against his skin made it difficult. So did the quiet movement of bugs and small animals in the trees around him. And the knowledge that he'd be sleeping on the hard ground again tonight.

Never thought I'd go through this again.

He made his way back to Cami, his mind embroiled in the past. "The last time I fought in the water like that, I was the only one who came back to the surface." He hadn't meant to speak, to divulge one of his many sins, but the words sprang up and wouldn't be denied.

Cami looked at him a long moment. "How old were you?"

No use closing the door on that memory. He wasn't sure he could even if he tried. Luca didn't have to close his eyes to immerse himself in that morning, of being yanked from his cell and dragged outside. No weapons handed down that time. Just him, dressed only in a pair of shorts, and the other kid, who looked much the same. Too skinny, too afraid, too determined not to die. The fight hadn't been quick, and the moment the icy water closed over his head ... Luca shuddered. "Ten. Maybe eleven. The weeks and months blurred together while we were in hell."

She nodded, all business. "You survived."

Would she still look at him like that if she knew how many kids had their lives ended by him in those years? He must have earned something of a reputation, because the fights came more and more often toward the end, the audience of suited businessmen approaching the numbers of an actual crowd. Luca knew that fighting pits weren't the only thing they'd peddled in, but he'd been lucky in a way.

He almost laughed. *Lucky?* It sure as hell didn't feel like that. "Some days I wonder if it was worth it." If he'd gone down in the first fight ... Yeah, he'd be dead, but he also wouldn't have to carry this weight, day in and day out.

She gave a sad smile. "That's because you didn't lose your soul in the process."

"Don't be so sure about that. Maybe I didn't have any control over what went down in that place, but I *have* had control since then. I'm not a good man, and I've done shit that is flat out unforgivable."

She didn't speak again until they'd found a good spot to stop. Cami pulled out a med kit and ordered him to the ground with an imperial motion of her fingers. As she examined his wound, she finally spoke. "You survived. Before you got out of there and after. There are no saints in this world. If a person claims otherwise, they're selling something."

He wasn't so sure about that. Not anymore. Cami might not be as innocent as he'd originally thought, but she was a good person. She hadn't killed anyone, hadn't dragged herself through life with blackmail, lying, and cheating, all in the name of revenge.

He had.

He'd do worse before this was over.

14

C ami had never stitched a live wound before. Embroidery? Yes, because of course being a princess meant she had to learn that outdated technique of biding her time that women used before they had access to the internet. She'd resented those lessons as a child, had been more than grateful to leave them behind when she was finally old enough to argue and win with her father.

Look at her now.

It turned out that skin was nothing like cloth, and embroidery did not prepare her for what it took to stitch Luca's wound back together. He'd brushed off her questions about the slash on his forearm, but there was no denying the shoulder would needed stitches to hold it together.

So here they were.

He talked her through it in a low voice that was only the slightest bit strained with pain, instructing her how to clean the wound and the rest. By the time she sat back, a not-so-neat little row of stitches marked the wound. "It's going to scar."

"Another to add to the collection."

She wrapped it in a bandage and put her kit away. "We should get moving."

"Now's the time to bolt if you're going to. You might actually get away."

Cami didn't roll her eyes, but it was a near thing. "I'll bolt if you agree to engage your beacon and get someone with actual medical experience to look at that." She nodded at his shoulder. "Infection is a real risk on this island."

"Guess we're stuck then." He climbed to his feet, not nearly as fluid as he'd been yesterday, and pulled his pack over his good shoulder. He caught her looking and lowered his brows. "Don't you dare offer to carry this."

"Wouldn't dream of it." That was exactly what she'd been trying to figure out—how to take that burden from him for a little while. Cami glanced at the sky, barely visible between the intertwining branches and vines. "We're more than halfway through the Hunt. Three competitors down."

"Four."

She glanced at him. "What?"

"Four down. There was an altercation on the beach with our friend Vann."

"An altercation," she repeated. "I see."

"I told you I'm not a good guy, Cami." He started away from her, seemingly picking a direction at random.

She watched him for a moment, and then followed. "You know, you're not exactly putting together a good case for working with you until the end of this Hunt. You keep telling me that you're not a good guy. It's enough to have a woman doubting her choice to have really hot cave sex with you."

He shot her a glare over his shoulder and, god help her, she laughed. "That expression is quite forbidding, yes, but it might work better if you hadn't made me come like a dozen times in that cute little pool behind the waterfall."

"Cami—"

"I get it." She cut in before he could give her yet another well-meaning lecture on what a terrible person he was. "I'm playing the part of the fool, but I do understand. Your allegiance isn't—and never will be—to me. Just like mine can't be to you. It puts us at an impasse that will no doubt blow up in our faces on the last day of the hunt, but in the meantime, there's no reason to repeatedly remind me that I'm being an idiot for sticking by you for a few days."

"You're insufferable," Luca grumbled.

"You say the sweetest things." She had to fight to keep her smile in place, though. Luca might be the king of mixed signals since she met him, but she knew better than to believe the lie their bodies told them. Words—thoughts, plans, alliances—held more weight than something as fickle as chemistry, and no matter how much she liked the way they fit together physically, there was no future for her and Luca. He would betray her to win this thing. Or she would do the same to him for the same reason.

Neither one of them would forgive that betrayal.

They walked for a long time, and she was content to let the silence stretch out. Better to hear if someone else approached if they weren't making enough noise to summon the other competitors. She had no idea what kind of skillset the remaining people brought, but Cami had to assume they'd put in at least some training before throwing in their lots to compete in the Wild Hunt. She couldn't afford to underestimate them.

Luca moved through the trees as if he was one with them. He might hate it out here, but whatever lessons he'd learned as a child in that horrible place had stuck. The man made even less noise that Cami did.

There were only three competitors left. Dolph and Liam and Edward. Surely that meant she could secure this victory? Again, her gaze slid to Luca. He was the wild card. Would he wait to make his move until the last day? Or would he try before then?

"Stop looking at me like that."

"Like what?"

He didn't turn around. "Like you're wondering if I'll notice if you take off tonight. I'll notice, Cami, and I'll come for you."

She shivered in a way that wasn't entirely unpleasant. "Pass."

"This island is full of dangers."

Oh good lord, she'd thought they'd move beyond this. She *knew* this island was full of dangers, just like she *knew* Luca wasn't an upstanding citizen, just like she *knew* what she risked by competing. His insistence at seeing her as something fragile and needing to be guided was enough to have her stalking up to poke him in his good shoulder. "That's enough of that."

"Enough of what?" His tone said the question was merely to placate her, and that only had her anger spiking hotter.

"*You* are insufferable. Do I have to remind you that of the four people no longer in this competition, *I* managed two of them—without your help?"

He stopped and turned to face her. "You wouldn't have managed Envy alone."

It didn't matter that he was probably right on that score. He kept treating her ... Treating her the way the people back in Thalania did. As if she was the slightly stupider, much less sturdy, and infinitely less capable version of her broth-ers. "You can fuck right off."

"Are we really going to go through this song and dance again? You can't run away from me because I'll find you. You might as well accept my help—"

Cami kissed him. It was the only way to shut him up, or at least that's what she told herself as he staggered back a step until a nearby tree stopped their motion and held them steady. That space of a breath was the only hesitation in Luca. He spun them, divesting her of her pack in the process, and pinned her against the tree. And then he took control. He dug his hand into her hair and tilted her head back, punishing her with his mouth.

She wasn't in the mood to be punished.

Cami grabbed the waistband of his pants and yanked him closer. "I am so mad at you."

"I got that," he growled against her lips.

She rubbed him through her pants. He was large and hard against her palm, and she had every intention of ...

But then Luca had never cared much for Cami's inten-tions. He spun her around and waited until she caught herself on the tree to shove her pants to her knees. "You think you're in control. You're not."

He palmed her between her thighs, his hand careful despite his rough words. If ever there was a moment that summed up Luca, it was this one. Angry and muttering dark words against the back of her neck, but still touching her with a borderline reverence. She pushed back against the strength of his body at her back, needing him, and he answered by sliding two fingers into her. Doing it out here, frustrated and in the open, was so much hotter than she could have dreamed. Cami clung to the tree and pushed back, taking him deeper yet. "Yes, like that."

"Impatient."

"Frustrated," she corrected.

Luca gave that dark chuckle she loved so much. "Can't have that." He stroked her clit. "This doesn't end how you want, little princess. There is no happily ever after. There is no *anything* after this."

She hated the words even as she loved what he was doing to her body. Pleasure rose in waves, nearly drowning out the truth. "I don't believe in happily ever after."

"Liar," he murmured against her temple. "You want to paint me in a soft light and pretend I'm something I'm not. It won't work. I'll just hurt you in the end."

Her breath sobbed from her throat, but she refused to bend in this. "Luca?"

"Yeah?"

"Shut up and make me come. The only thing I want from you right now is an orgasm." *Liar*, her mind whispered, but she ignored it. No matter what he thought—what a small, secret part of her thought—she didn't actually believe that they had future together.

She couldn't afford to.

Luca responded her to words, his fingers keeping up that delicious stroking in exactly the way she needed to come apart at the seams. She wanted to hold on to that moment, to unspool time and create a space where nothing real could touch them. It wasn't meant to be. He pressed down on her clit and she came with a low cry, only his hold on her keeping her off the ground.

And then there was nothing left to do but breathe.

What are we doing?

She knew the answer, even if she didn't want to admit it.

Making a mistake.

Luca stepped back and she righted her clothing. Her

chest felt tight and she really, really didn't want to examine why. Cami was many things, but irrational wasn't one of them. She'd worked *hard* to be impervious, and she couldn't afford to falter now. She smoothed down her shirt. "I get it, Luca. I really do. We don't have a future, and this is just fucking, and your only loyalty is to your people. You really don't have to keep reminding me every ten seconds." She finally worked up the courage to look him full in the face, and his expression was just as conflicted as the feelings slicing through her chest. "Or were you trying to remind yourself?"

"I never expected this to be so fucking complicated." Luca glanced away and ran his hand over his face. "Cami ..."

"As delightful as this show has been, I'm going to step in now," a voice said almost directly behind Cami.

Before she could turn, a hand closed over her shoulder ...

And a blade pressed against her throat.

Luca held his breath as Liam Neale stepped behind Cami, his blade at her throat. He looked like he'd seen some shit since they were dropped on the island. Dried blood caked the side of his face, and he moved with a slight limp. None of that detracted from the fact *he had a blade at Cami's neck*. Luca held up his hands slowly. "Let's be reasonable."

"Reasonable stopped being a possibility the second we landed in this nightmare." Even Liam's voice was different, raspy and holding a deep rage Luca understood all too well. Liam took a step back and then another, dragging Cami with him. He towered over her smaller frame, could easily do her lasting damage, even by accident.

"What do you want?"

Liam stopped and really looked at him. "You act like this isn't the whole point of the Hunt. Would you be this protective if it was Kenzie in danger?"

Shock froze Luca in his tracks. He had used Kenzie's real name casually with Cami, but that was a different situation. *No one* knew the Horsemen's true identities. Even with Luca originating in Thalania and having that dog and pony show arriving at the island as a result, there was still a relatively small pool of people who knew his given name. *Only* his.

No one knew the others.

They'd worked hard to ensure that was the case, to banish their flawed selves and project a public persona so dangerous, it would warn off smaller threats while the Horsemen grew in power. They succeeded.

And yet this man, this Irish mob lackey from Boston, somehow knew Kenzie's name.

"Get her name out of your mouth."

Liam smiled bitterly. "And *that* is why I'm here."

He wanted Kenzie.

No.

Fuck no.

Luca started forward, only to pull up short when Liam shifted the blade against Cami's throat. "Remember yourself, Famine. I don't want to hurt her, but I will if it comes to that." Desperation and determination laced his tone, a potent combination.

For her part, Cami remained eerily calm. "What do you want with Kenzie?"

"That's between us."

Lies. This man wanted what every man wanted from Kenzie. To possess her, to have her on their arm, to shove her into a little box in their life where she would be a trapped thing and die a little more each day. His sister had fought too hard for her freedom to submit, to be *forced* to submit.

They all had.

Luca took another step. "She's not for you."

"I repeat—that's between us."

Cami sent Luca a sharp look that he couldn't decipher. She placed a soft hand on Liam's wrist. "If you care about her, do you really think this is the way to go about it?" She turned in Liam's grasp and he let her. Luca couldn't see her expression from where he stood, but he had a feeling it was all sweetness and sincerity. Her voice radiated sympathy. "Wouldn't it be better to—" Cami hit him in the throat. She was too close to do the kind of damage that would be preferable, but Luca jumped forward and knocked the knife out of Liam's hand. Cami ducked out of the way, and Luca punched him in the face. Once. Twice. A third time.

Liam hit the ground, his hands at his throat.

"Did you crush his windpipe?"

"Of course not." Cami reached down, fished Liam's beacon out of his shirt, grabbed one of his hands, and pressed his finger to engage it. "You should really just talk to her, Liam. She might surprise you."

"Now's not the time for relationship advice." Luca chose not to say that Kenzie would set herself on fire before she'd have the kind of conversation Liam seemed to be seeking. It was a problem for another day, and they had bigger concerns.

There were only two competitors left, and they were both the Bookkeeper's men.

Well, technically there are three competitors left.

He looked around, belatedly registering that he hadn't been worried about cameras in far too long. Not since the cavern. They'd walked and spoken and fucked around and it was entirely possible—probable even—that most of what had happened since they left the cavern had been witnessed.

Shit.

"We need to move."

"Agreed." Cami scooped up her pack and started unerringly north, leaving a gasping Liam in her wake. She didn't look back to ensure Luca followed her, didn't give Liam another concern now that he was removed from the competition.

Fuck, but Luca loved her.

He rocked back on his heels, the inconvenient realization nearly sending him to his knees. *No, you're wrong. You want her, and yeah, you respect that she's a lot more capable than you ever gave her credit for, but ... Love? Impossible.*

Isn't it?

"Luca?"

He gave himself a shake and followed, ignoring the murderous look Liam sent him. The man would have to figure his shit out, but Luca would sure as hell be warning Kenzie. He glanced around. Or maybe she already knew. If Liam knew enough to know her name ...

A worry for another day. He couldn't afford to dwell on it, not with the end of the Hunt bearing down on them and his betrayal sitting like a rock in his stomach. The very thing he'd wanted to avoid—Dolph getting his hands on Cami—was the only outcome that wouldn't completely fuck Amarante's plan beyond all recognition. *Their* plan. They needed the Bookkeeper, and they'd never been this close to tempting him onto the island before. If they blew this chance, it could be years before they worked up to it again.

It might never happen.

And all the while, more children would go missing, prey to the sick games those bastards liked to play.

No.

Loving Cami couldn't push him to stray from this path. The stakes were too high, there were people depending on him that he couldn't let down. Children he'd never met, their innocence burned away by a trauma he knew all too well. What was that compared to Cami's inevitable hate?

It shouldn't even be a consideration. He knew that. Even being tempted to change the plan was the height of selfishness, and unforgivable in its own way.

They walked for close to an hour before Cami stopped and faced him. "Why didn't you let Yael come to you?"

Luca stopped short. "What?"

"I get not wanting to go back to Thalania. I understood that even before I met you. I think everyone did, to some degree. What I *don't* understand is why you never let Yael come here to see you, not even once. She's your grandmother."

He didn't want to talk about this, didn't want to drag out the ugliness even further. It felt like ever since he'd entered the Wild Hunt, the only thing *hunting* was his past hunting him. He still answered her. It was the least he could do considering what came next. Luca looked around, but by some stroke of luck, they weren't any cameras present. Maybe that was why he answered Cami. "She's a woman I could barely remember."

"If you don't want to answer, then don't answer. But don't lie to me. You were ten when you were taken—old enough to have *some* memory of her."

He sighed. "You know her."

"I know her," she confirmed.

"I spent most of my first decade with her in the Nibley

house. My parents were more into playing petty politics in Thalania than they were in raising a kid, so she was all I had. Most of my important memories were tied to her." He didn't want to keep going, didn't want to speak this unspeakable thing, but Cami simply stood there with an open expression, waiting for the truth, and he could give her nothing less. "I couldn't face her. Not after what happened, what I did, what was done to me."

Cami didn't say anything, so he kept going, trying to find the words to make her understand. "Yael—my grandmother —values strength and cunning above all else. Those are the gods she worships. She drilled into me from birth that we use those skills to protect those around us. It's our duty, the reason we were born into a family of influence." He finally looked at Cami. "I didn't protect those kids. I killed ... So many of them. In the end, I couldn't even protect myself. If it wasn't for Amarante, I would have died in one of those pits, too."

"You were *ten* when they took you, Luca. You can't honestly be expected to act the part of a savior when you were a child."

"I was a Nibley." He said it simply, a truth that used to be *his* truth. "I should have figured out a way. *She* would have figured out a way."

Cami stared at him a long time. "Promise me something."

He already knew what she wanted. "It won't solve anything. It's been too long." He didn't even know what he'd say if he was in the same room as his grandmother again. They were strangers to each other. Worse than strangers, really, because they used to be family.

"Luca ..." Cami took a deep breath. "She's dying. She has

less than a year. If you don't see her soon, you won't have the chance to do it at all."

Yael ... dying?

It seemed impossible. His grandmother had always been larger than life, both when Luca was a child and later as an adult when she'd set her sights on bringing him home. She hadn't succeeded, but she'd tried for far longer than anyone could have anticipated. She was *still* trying if Cami's presence on the island was any indication. "I can't promise that I'll see her."

"Promise me you'll consider it—*really* consider it."

He started to shut her down, but forced himself to check his knee-jerk reaction. He could promise to consider it, truly consider it. It was the least he could do. "I promise."

"Thank you." She crossed to him and took his hands. "I know it doesn't guarantee anything, but thank you for at least considering it. I think she might surprise you if you give her half a chance."

He couldn't consider for long, not if Yael was truly edging into the end of her life.

Luca put it away. He couldn't do anything in the next few days, not until the Hunt was over, and after that things would move quickly. Once the Bookkeeper was dealt with and they had their next steps mapped out ... Then he'd see. "Let's keep moving."

"Okay."

It was only later, as the sun edged toward the horizon, that Luca thought about the fact Cami hadn't once asked him what the plan was.

15

Cami lay in the dark and listened to Luca climb to his feet. She'd known this was coming. Maybe not *this*, exactly, but something. He'd been too quiet all day. As tempted as she was to chalk it up to the uncomfortable conversation about Yael, she knew better, the real turning point was when they knocked Liam out of the Hunt.

There were only two other competitors left, and they were both part of the alliance she'd noted. If Luca wasn't meant to win, then it was only logical that one of them had to.

It still hurt to hear him walk away from their makeshift camp, and it fucking *hurt* to know he didn't trust her enough to tell her his plans.

Would she have altered her course if he had?

Cami had no answers. Playing the what-if game served no purpose. She couldn't think about what might have happened, because she had to deal with what *had* happened. Luca left her. More, she had no doubt that the other men would find her sooner, rather than later, and likely at Luca's hand.

It cut deeper than she could have anticipated, and she *had* anticipated it.

She lay there for a long time, long after she should have moved, considering her next step. If there was a trap, she had no intention of walking into it, but charging out into the night was a good way to end up in a pit or a cage. Instead, Cami waited for first light to rise and quickly pack her things up.

He should have asked me to help.

If he'd just trusted me ...

What would she have done? Given up her chance at freedom for him?

Cami paused. Maybe. In the end, she lived a life of privilege and even if she hadn't found other avenues to accomplish what she wanted—a way to make both a clean break and maintain her relationship with her family—she wasn't selfish enough to ignore what Luca's aims would accomplish.

The people who stole him away from his family as a child were never caught. Neither were the monsters who frequented that place. They hadn't simply gone out of business and morphed into upstanding citizens because they shut down one of their locations. No, they'd moved shop, and likely had several times in the intervening years. Who knew how many children they'd hurt in the meantime?

How could her freedom—her happiness—compare with that?

Luca hadn't trusted her, had set her up to act the part of a fool and ...

Cami stopped short.

Did it matter?

To her heart ... absolutely. Her chest felt like he'd carved out part of it with a rusty spoon. Breathing hurt. Moving hurt. Everything hurt. She wanted to track him, to yell at him, to make him see what a fool he was being.

This wasn't just about Cami's feelings, though. Even if she didn't like the means, there was more at stake, had *always* been more at stake. Was she really willing to burn it all to ash simply because Luca had somehow gotten close enough to break her heart?

Unbidden, Yael's voice echoed through her thoughts. *We protect, Princess. It's our role in life, no matter what path our feet take.*

Protect.

She's always taken that to mean her people, the citizens of Thalania, but what if Cami's path actually lay elsewhere? Wasn't that what she always wanted, what she'd fought so hard for? This was her chance to ensure it happened, to actually do some real good in the world.

She just had to give up everything to do it.

Without another thought, she turned and headed for the northern extraction point. If she was going to be caught, she wanted to be in their possession as little time as possible. It was still a risk, and the thought of all the ways it could go wrong left her breathless. She didn't have a better option. Maybe if Luca had stayed, they could have planned it better, but he didn't.

She was on her own.

Cami let anger guide her steps. She forced herself not to move quietly, to blunder through the trees as if this was her first time away from civilization. God, she hated this, hated that she was reduced to this, hated that Luca put her in this position in the first place.

If he'd just *talked* to her ...

No use going down that rabbit hole of grief yet again. He

hadn't talked to her. He'd left to ensure his goals were real-ized. He'd betrayed her. End of story.

Hours passed as she walked in a meandering path, weaving back and forth in sweeping arcs that even someone who'd never tracked a person in their life could follow. The faint light of morning shifted to sticky heat and a humidity thick enough to choke her. She gradually made her way to the coast again, emerging from the jungle in nearly the same spot she'd entered it a few days ago. She was a mile, maybe a little less, south of the extraction point. From this position, she could even see the smaller island perched to the north-east, a glittering gem of paradise. A reminder of the influence the Horsemen brought to the game, of how none of this was ever left up to chance.

Of how Cami never actually stood a chance of winning.

Shame clawed through her chest, merging with humilia-tion. They'd made a fool out of her, something she could have forgiven if not for how Luca *personally* made a fool out of her. There were cameras all over this island. Had he intentionally seduced her ...

No.

No.

She couldn't think like that. She was angry and hurting, and it swayed her thinking. Luca might be an asshole, but he wasn't a monster. No matter how he self-identified because of his past. He hadn't wanted to want her—he'd made *that* more than clear. The betrayal was planned, the sex was not. Cami had to believe that.

She swiped her forearm across her forehead. How close could she get to the extraction point without it being suspicious?

She never got the answer.

A man stalked out of the trees, taking nearly the same

path she had. Tracking her. He was covered in camouflage paint, smears or green and brown and black that masked his tan skin and blond hair. It didn't mask the menace rolling off him in waves. He smiled, a shock of white teeth against the muddied colors of his skin. "Hello, Princess."

Dolph.

She stopped thinking.

She stopped planning.

Cami dropped her pack and bolted across the sand.

She barely made it three steps before he was on her, snagging her around the waist and yanking her back against his body. "Now, now. You can't leave the party before it even starts." He shifted and she had no doubt in her mind that he was marking the sun's location in the sky. "We're close enough to the extraction point that we can afford to take our time." He lowered his face and whispered in her ear. "It's almost like you wanted this."

She froze, cold truth striking her in the face. All this time, she'd imagined herself a fox or some other clever animal. One to be underestimated as she tricked and manipulated her way to a win.

The truth?

She was a rabbit with her leg in a trap.

It took everything she had to keep her voice from shaking. "If you touch me, I'll kill you."

"I'm touching you right now, Princess." He squeezed her hip as if to remind her exactly how trapped she was. Worse, she could feel evidence of his arousal against her back.

No.

She had almost made her peace with losing the Hunt. She would *not* make her peace with this. The price was too high.

Cami took a slow breath and forced her body to go soft.

Her knife was still in its sheath at her hip, but if she killed him, that would mean this whole thing was for nothing. There had to be a better way. If she hurt him badly enough that she could guarantee she'd reach the extraction point first … The time hadn't run out. Even if she was there, she wouldn't win, but by the time he caught up with her, *he* would win.

It wasn't a great plan. It wasn't even a good plan.

It was still the only shot she had.

Thigh wound, she decided. As long as she didn't hit the femoral artery, he should live. Cami started to turn in his arms, but he tightened his grip. "Ah ah. It's better this way."

Do not panic. Breathe. Stay soft.

It was the hardest thing she'd ever done. She shivered, and that reaction was apparently exactly what Dolph was waiting for. His hand went to the front of her pants.

A switch flipped in her brain and everything went sharp and clear. Cami grabbed her knife and stabbed him in the thigh, twisting it as she withdrew. He cursed but didn't let her go.

She stabbed him again. Then she switched hands and stabbed his other leg three times in quick succession.

Dolph fell to the ground behind her and she didn't pause to look back and check on the damage. She just ran. She ran as if the very hounds of hell were on her heels. They might as well have been. If Dolph caught her again, he'd kill her this time. She had no illusions about that.

She risked a look over her shoulder. She couldn't help it.

He wasn't on the ground any more. He staggered after her, a splotchy trail of red in his wake and her murder in his eyes.

Faster, Cami.

L<small>UCA HAD</small> every intention of finding and dealing with Dolph —permanently. It was a risk. Killing Dolph left only one competitor—Edward—and if the man wasn't savvy enough to track Cami, it would all be for naught. He didn't care. It was worth it to ensure Dolph didn't get his hands on Cami. Even now, even while orchestrating things so that she would lose the Hunt, he couldn't let something happen to her. Not something permanent. No matter what she thought about the future, Cami would be okay. She had more resources than most people—and that was without the inheritance and the influence of Thalania behind her.

Again and again, he'd misjudged her and underestimated her.

It didn't matter anymore. He'd made the only call he could, would see this through to the end. Cami would hate Luca. There was no outcome for this Hunt where she *didn't* hate Luca.

He just hoped it was worth it.

But after a day spent fruitlessly searching for signs of the Bookkeeper's people, he came up with nothing. There were only forty-eight hours left in the Hunt. He didn't have time to search the entire length of the island. In all his planning, it never occurred to Luca that Dolph and his man might not find her. That they might be unprepared for the challenges of this Hunt. Right now, they could be stuck in one of the traps littering this place and Luca would never know. It wasn't like they had some kind of announcement when a competitor was removed from the game.

Damn it, he never should have left Cami.

He'd fucked this all up.

Luca turned and headed back toward the camp they'd

made that night. He hadn't actually wandered that far, moving in ever widening circles, so he reached it quickly. Naturally, Cami had long since gone. Even expecting that, disappointment soured his stomach. Had he really thought she'd sit idly and wait for ... What? For him to come back? To be taken?

He knew better.

Where to go now?

His plan lay in shambles. His intentions were all over the place. He didn't know what the fuck he was supposed to do. None of this was *supposed* to happen.

Cami would move toward the extraction point, wouldn't she? She'd already proved adept at hiding and ambushing as required, and she stood a good chance of waiting out the remaining two days if she stayed in one place where she knew the traps and the area. Would she stick with that plan? Or would she strike deeper into the interior of the island?

He didn't know.

He didn't fucking *know*.

A scream echoed in the distance.

Luca didn't think. He reacted, turning and racing in the direction of that cry. North. Toward the coast. He shouldn't have been able to hear it at this distance, not with the jungle dampening the sound, but he'd spent nearly a week attuned to Cami's every breath. He would know her voice anywhere, even risen in a panicked cry.

Cami was *panicking*.

Fear gave him wings, and he practically flew over the ground as he sprinted through the trees. If she was hurt, it was his fault. If she was hurt ... He poured on the speed, his breath rasping in and out in a cadence he couldn't escape. *My fault. My fault. My fault.*

Luca burst out of the trees and shot onto the beach. He

skidded to a halt, trying to get his bearings. She hadn't screamed again ... Maybe he'd gone too far ...

But no.

A few hundred yards up the beach Cami ran for her life, a bleeding Dolph chasing her down. He staggered and seemed to wince with every step, but that wasn't slowing him down any. He'd be on her in seconds. Luca took off after them, running faster than he ever had. It wouldn't be enough. He knew it wouldn't be enough.

Dolph took Cami down in a flying tackle that sent them rolling into the surf. He made a move Luca couldn't see and then a knife went flying away from them. Dolph rose to his knees and dragged Cami farther into the water.

Luca reached them just as he dunked her under. He grabbed the man by the throat and yanked him out of the water, bringing Cami with them. Dolph released her in surprise, but it was too late. Luca drove him to the ground and delivered a devastating punch to his jaw. And another. And another.

Until Cami shoved him forcibly enough to send him slumping off the fallen man. "Stop!"

Luca spun on her. "He was going to drown you!"

"He was going to do more than that." Her chest heaved with every breath, but she still stared him down as if this was all his fault.

She was right.

"Cami—"

"I don't want to hear it." She cautiously reached down and pressed her fingers to Dolph's neck. "He's still alive. Good."

Luca couldn't believe what he was hearing. "*Good?*"

"Help me." She pulled one of Dolph's arms over her shoulder. "Hurry, before he wakes up."

"What the fuck are you doing?"

Cami barely glanced at him. "This is what you wanted, isn't it? He has to win. Not you. Not me. Help me get him to the extraction point and then I'll take care of the rest."

Yeah, he really couldn't believe what he was hearing. "It's a trick."

"Luca, I swear to all that's holy, I will kick your ass if you make me drag this psychopath all the way to the extraction point. *Help me.*"

Numb, he pulled Dolph up and wedged himself under the other man's arm. He took most of the man's weight as they staggered to their feet and started down the beach. He started to ask her questions half a dozen times during that hellish walk, but each time Luca changed his mind. Better to get them to their destination and then worry about the rest. He kept an eye out while they moved, but the other competitor didn't appear to be in the area.

It was only when they dropped Dolph to the sand that Luca turned to her. They stood in the little indent that couldn't quite be called a bay. The smaller island lay directly across the water from there, only about a mile away. So close and yet so far. He cleared his throat. "Why?"

"You'd know why if you put absolutely any thought into it." She refused to look at him, crouching down to pull Dolph's beacon from around his neck. "How do I trigger this for the win?"

"The bottom part detaches, and there's a button inside." Another beacon, though this one would signal to everyone in the casino and watching that someone had the Stag. It had never happened in the history of the Wild Hunt.

It shouldn't be happening now. "Cami—"

"No!" She stood and lowered her voice. "No. You made your choice, Luca. I'm just trying to abide by it." She still wouldn't look at him. "You should go. You don't want to be here when they show up to congratulate the winner."

He didn't want to leave. He wanted to explain to her why this had to be done. Except ... Apparently he didn't need to explain shit. She'd already divined out his intent and she'd made good on it, even if he hadn't been able to. *I fucked this all up*. "I'm sorry."

"No, you're not. You'd do the same thing over again without a second thought." She turned to look at the small island and took a deep breath. Cami pushed the button and bent to loop it around Dolph's neck again. She turned a quick circle, her expression pensive, and then walked several paces away and dropped to the ground like a puppet who'd had its strings cut.

Luca looked at the scene. It appeared to be almost exactly what he'd found when he burst out of the trees—a struggle in which Dolph had half drowned Cami and Cami had stabbed Dolph until he'd passed out from blood loss.

The only thing missing was Luca's absence. "I'm sorry," he said again.

He forced himself to walk away.

16

C ami lay on the beach, half in the water, for less
than an hour before the sound of a boat cut
through the quiet. And then War—Kenzie—was
there, striding across the sand with a forbidding look on her
face. She glanced at Cami, examined Dolph, and muttered
something under her breath. A few seconds later, she
leaned down over Cami, blocking out the late afternoon
sun. "You can get up now. His win has been recorded."

Cami opened her eyes. What was she supposed to do?
Thank Kenzie for the fact she didn't have to be hauled into
the boat like some kind of dead animal, carted back as a
prize. Cold flashed through her. "My role stops here."

"Yes, it does." Kenzie took her hand and hauled her to
her feet.

Cami's legs buckled, but she forced them straight. She'd
arrived on the island on her own power, and she'd leave the
same way. Really, it would be like the Wild Hunt never
happened.

With that depressing thought weighing her down, she
walked past Dolph and climbed into the waiting boat. It was

the same one Kenzie had brought her over on the first night. Had that only been five days ago? It felt like a small lifetime.

Kenzie slapped Dolph a few times, and he roused. "What?"

"Get up, asshole. You won. Unless you want to lie there on the sand and bleed to death."

It took a little doing, but eventually Dolph joined her in the boat. He watched her with those eerie eyes. "You got lucky, Princess."

She huddled in the blanket she'd found under her seat. It wasn't technically cold, but she couldn't stop shivering. "Sure doesn't feel like luck."

He tightened the makeshift bandages on his thighs and laughed. "Don't worry. We'll pick up where we left off the first chance I get."

Fear flashed through her, and she was too tired to keep it off her face. She *hated* that he made her feel afraid, hated that this entire charade was necessary. "If you touch me again, I'll kill you."

"You'll try. It'll be like foreplay."

Kenzie slapped him upside the back of his head. "Fuck off, Dolph. Don't be a sore winner." She guided the boat across the water at a dizzying speed. And then they were entering the harbor where a writhing mass of people waited like a glittering flock of birds in their fancy clothing.

A direct counterpart to how bedraggled Cami was.

"Stay in the boat," Kenzie murmured. "My brother will scoop you up after the adoring masses follow us back to Pleasure."

Right. Because they weren't there for Cami. She'd played her part, and now Dolph got to walk the route of the winner to collect his favor from Death. She'd planned this when she walked onto that beach a few hours ago. Maybe Cami hadn't intended for it to fall out like *this*, but she'd still chosen this path.

That it was the truth didn't make it sting any less.

She sat silently in the gently bobbing boat as Dolph struggled to his feet and followed Kenzie onto the dock. He had to be dizzy from blood loss, but he managed to power through it and they walked up the cobblestone path toward the casino perched overlooking the bay.

Cami was so incredibly tired.

She blinked and the light changed. Had she fallen asleep? A shadow fell over her, and she flinched before she caught herself. She looked up quickly, her heart in her throat, but it wasn't Luca standing over her. Of course it wasn't Luca. He would still be back on the island, waiting to be collected. He couldn't possibly be *here*. She certainly didn't want him here, either.

An Asian man offered a hand. "Come on."

It took her several precious seconds to place him. Pestilence. The name was laughable when paired with his strong body and attractive face, but she supposed someone had to take the role. More than that, Cami had heard rumors that no one was safe from Pestilence if he turned his attention their way. Funds went missing, *identities* went missing. Anything that was stored electronically was fair game, and these days *everything* was stored electronically. Cami might not always appreciate the role she'd been born into, but she couldn't imagine waking up one day to find that record of everything from her birth to her property to her bank account ... gone. She shivered.

"You're safe, Princess."

Right. Because she'd played the part they set out for her. She couldn't dredge up any anger over that. Maybe tomorrow she'd be mad. Right now, she just wanted a shower and a bed.

Cami slipped her hand into his and allowed him to guide her out of the boat. The dock felt strange under her boots after being on the water, but she adjusted quickly. "Thank you." She tried to take back her hand, but Pestilence maintained his hold.

"I …" He gave her hand a squeeze and released her. "Thank you. My sisters will never say it, and I can't speak to Famine's motivations, but thank you for what you did."

She looked around, but they were alone on the dock. The revelers had moved on. "There's nothing to thank me for. Anyone would have done it if they knew the stakes."

"No, they wouldn't." He offered his arm, the same kind of old world move her oldest brother would pull, and Cami instinctively laid her hand on his forearm.

It wasn't until they reached the path and turned south, toward Pain, that she realized she shouldn't trust him just because she'd trusted Luca. *Trusted* being the operative word. "You aren't going to toss me into a dungeon or something, are you?"

"No." He paused long enough that she thought that might be the entirety of his answer, but then he said, "Things will be tumultuous in Pleasure for the next few days. It would be better—safer—if you stayed in Pain for the duration. I can arrange transport if you need to leave before then."

"I don't." She spoke too quickly, giving herself away.

He didn't react the way either of his sisters would have. No arched eyebrow. No sharp comment. Just a small nod. "In that case, I've taken the liberty of arranging rooms for you in Pain. All your belongings have already been transported there."

There was nothing else to say. She didn't really want to go back to the villa, and if her things were already in the new rooms, that was enough to keep her moving.

That and the fact that she'd be an entire island away from Luca and whatever plot he and his siblings were playing out. It was better that way. As Pestilence said, she'd played her part and played it well. It didn't matter if she'd only made the choice this morning. She'd seen it through.

They reached Pain quickly, and walking inside was nearly enough to distract Cami from her misery. The northern casino was all glitz and glam and decadent delights. She hadn't thought much about what Pain would look like, but she'd assumed it would be dark and filled with … Actually, Cami wasn't sure what she'd thought.

Reality was something else altogether.

It was downright minimalist. Low lights and strong dark colors, like some kind of high-end gentleman's club. The main room looked like a lounge, and there was a row of doors lining the opposite wall. The plaques above them listed blackjack and several kinds of poker. High stakes games.

Pestilence guided her to the left, down a wide hallway with oil paintings that could only be classified as erotic. Cami flushed, but she didn't look away. They were beautiful, each depicting a different part of the body. A muscled shoulder. A breast. The flare of a hip. An ankle. "I've never seen this artist before."

"That's because the only place in the world with access to them is the Island of Ys."

Easy enough to read between the lines. The artist was one of the four. She didn't ask which one. In the end, it didn't matter. Cami would come back and study them later.

She didn't have the capacity to wonder overmuch about them in her current state.

"You're free to move about as you like." Pestilence stopped in front of a deep red door and unlocked it with an honest-to-god key. He opened the door and passed it over. "Both private and play rooms are unlocked unless they're rented out, so you don't have to worry about stumbling into something you'd rather not witness. If you like to watch, however, there are observation rooms set up just around the corner that look into the rooms where both parties have consented to an audience." Again, no expression on his face to indicate what he thought of that. It was all just business. "There's a full menu to order from on the table, but if you'd prefer to cook, we can bring in whatever you need."

"Thank you." Exhaustion rolled over her, threatening to suck her under. She didn't care about food, didn't care about what were apparently sex rooms in this part of Pain, didn't care about anything but a shower and a bed and enough sleep to dim the pain pulsing in her chest.

"Someone will collect you when it's finished." He waited for her to step into the room and closed the door softly behind her.

She locked the door and leaned against it. Only then did his words penetrate. *When it's finished.*

When they'd enacted the first part of their revenge.

Luca strode into the hub and bypassed all three of his siblings on his way to his room. Kenzie started to say something, but Amarante stopped her with a hand on her shoulder. "We'll talk after you shower and change."

He didn't respond. What was there to say? They'd

accomplished what they wanted. All that was left to do was to focus on the next step and the next and the next. He'd never been so tired in his life. Luca stripped off his clothes and balled them up to shove into the garbage bag someone—probably Amarante—had left hanging on the doorknob to his bathroom. He wouldn't wear them again, could barely stand the sight of them and what they represented.

His betrayal.

After turning on the shower as hot as he could stand it, he stepped beneath the water. Then, and only then, did he allow himself to remember the look on Cami's face the last time he'd saw her. Remember how she'd kept her head even after Dolph had attacked her. Remember how *she'd* kept them on track when Luca would have faltered.

She knew he double-crossed her, and she'd still worked to see it through and sacrificed her win in the process.

Fuck, but he loved that woman.

Luca smiled bitterly. It didn't matter, couldn't matter, now any more than it had on the island. He had a role to play out and even if Cami was willing to be party to it, he couldn't ask that of her. That woman was destined for great things, whether she realized it or not. Asking her to stay in the shadows with him ...

But then, it didn't matter what he would or wouldn't ask her. No doubt she wanted nothing to do with him. She'd be on the next flight off the island, and maybe her charmed life wouldn't feel so flat now that she'd played a part in the Wild Hunt.

Maybe someday she'd forgive him.

He scrubbed his body down twice before he turned off the water and dried off quickly. No point to delay the next step. Luca threw on a pair of slacks and a button-up shirt, though he wanted to drop onto his mattress and sleep for twelve hours straight. Plenty of time for that later.

In theory.

His siblings were almost exactly where he'd left them. Ryu sat in front of the monitors, no doubt keeping an eye on Dolph. Amarante and Kenzie spoke quietly, but their conversation trailed off the second he stepped back into the room. Amarante gave one of her rare smiles. "Dolph just put out a call to his employer."

The Bookkeeper.

Luca exhaled. "Then it was worth it."

"You did well."

Even as he told himself he wouldn't ask, he said, "Cami?"

Amarante raised an eyebrow. "Princess Camilla Fitzcharles is occupying rooms in Pain until this is finished. Her every need will be seen to for the duration."

"Least we can do since we kind of fucked her over," Kenzie chimed in.

Luca started to turn, but then stopped himself. It didn't matter where Cami was or what *needs* she fulfilled in Pain. She wasn't his. He didn't get a say in her actions or her future.

He wanted a fucking say.

He scrubbed his hands over his face. "When will the Bookkeeper be here?"

"Tonight for the closing ceremony." Amarante's expression went contemplative. "He must be close, but we expected that. He played the odds too well not to believe his win is legitimate." She refocused on Luca. "Get some sleep or do something to bleed off that energy. I need you focused tonight. We have to present a unified front. We have to *be* a unified front."

That stung more than it had right to. "I'm fine, Te."

"No, you're not." No condemnation. Just a statement of fact. "You're all twisted up over that woman, and it's going to bleed over into this operation if you don't get your head on straight." She glanced at the slim watch on her wrist. "You have four hours. Figure it out."

"Easy for you to say."

Her dark eyes flashed and he got the impression of both Kenzie and Ryu edging away as Amarante bore down on him. She stopped a few inches away, her voice low and deadly. "We have all sacrificed to get here, Luca. *All* of us. You don't have the market cornered on misery. I'm sorry you got tangled up with the woman. I really am. If it helps, she will be compensated for her choice to help us." At his look, she shook her head. "Did you think we missed that?"

"I thought you didn't care."

Real hurt flickered in Amarante's eyes before she steeled her expression. "You know better, Luca. I might play the villain when I have to, but you of all people should know better."

He did. Damn it, he did. He took a breath and then another. He'd made his choice, same as the rest of them. Blaming Amarante for putting the whole thing into motion was like blaming the sky for being blue. They had always barreled down the path to this destination. His wavering determination couldn't be blamed on anyone but *him*. "I'm sorry." He was so twisted over Cami that every breath felt like he drove shards of glass into his chest.

She tapped his forehead gently with a single finger. "Do what you need to do to get your head on straight before the Bookkeeper gets here." She stepped back and hesitated. "She's safe, Luca. No matter how the next few days play out, she'll be kept out of it." It was as much of a concession from Amarante as he could expect to get.

"I'll be back before the ceremony." He left the room, painfully aware of the way all three of them watched him.

As if he was the loose cannon.

As if he might do something stupid to endanger everything they'd fought and sacrificed for.

The worst part? He wasn't sure their concern was unwarranted. Luca *felt* like a loose cannon. He wanted to punch something, to run, to do *something* to bleed out the horrible feeling clutching at his chest. He slipped out of one of the doors into an empty room, headed for the hall, and chose a direction at random.

Twenty minutes later, he looked up at the sweeping lines of Pain and knew he'd always been on his way there. No matter what his brain said, his body hadn't gotten the memo. It felt like an invisible cord attached him to Cami, vibrating with the need to see her, pulling him ever in her direction.

She hated him. She had to.

Luca stepped from the heat and into the icy air-conditioned building. Maybe if he saw her one last time, it would give them both closure. She could yell or throw things or deliver one of those devastatingly soft verbal cuts. He would stand there and bleed as was his due. Then they would be free to move on in separate directions, never to meet again.

His reasoning wouldn't stand up to any kind of examination, but luckily he didn't have to justify it to anyone but himself, and Luca wanted to see her again, even if it was destined to be a painful experience. At least then it would be over, any questions resolved.

Closure. It was only about closure.

One of the staff approached him the second he paused on the main floor, a young guy Kenzie had brought home with her after one of her trips. He gave a tight smile. "Mr. Pestilence said to give this to you." He held out a card.

Luca bit back a sigh and took it. "Thanks."

"My pleasure. Is there anything else I can do for you?"

"No, I'm good." He waited for the guy to walk away before he looked at the card. The handwriting wasn't Ryu's for obvious reasons, but the words were. *She's in The Rose Room.* Of course Ryu would divine his intentions even before he did. Luca slipped the card into his pocket and headed for the Rose Room.

When they'd built this place, they decided that room numbers weren't in line with the atmosphere they wanted to cultivate, so all the private rooms had names. Some were colors, some flowers, some birds. Fitting that Cami occupied the rose room. It'd been set up for someone who fancied themselves royalty. Everything was pristine and untouchable looking.

A lot like Cami looked when he'd first met her.

Now he knew better. He recognized the core strength beneath the surface, the one she intentionally hid. She was clever and brilliant and stronger than he could have dreamed. Maybe in another life they could have made it work.

It didn't matter now.

Maybe if he told himself that enough times, he'd actually believe it.

Luca stopped in front of the door to her room and hesitated. In the end, there was nothing to do but knock. Listening to soft footsteps approach was a special kind of misery, but it was no match for when she opened the door and he got his first look at her since the island.

She wore loose lounge pants and a flowing tank top that looked relaxed and put together, all that the same time.

Cami sucked in a breath and in that moment before she composed her expression, he saw a tangle of hurt and desire and anger. All of it directed at him. "What are you doing here?"

"I don't know." It didn't even occur to him to lie. "I guess I came to apologize."

Cami stared at him a long moment and finally nodded, almost to herself. "I guess you should come in, then."

17

Cami didn't know what she was supposed to say. She didn't know if she was angrier with Luca for betraying her ... or for not trusting her enough to understand that she'd make the same call if given half a chance.

That was a lie.

Cami knew exactly which one of those she was angriest about.

She stepped back into the room and waited for him to shut the door. He looked good, but he always seemed to look good to her. It didn't matter if he was clothed in suits or cargo pants and a T-shirt. It simply wasn't fair.

"Cami ..."

She crossed her arms over chest and waited. No matter how much she wanted to rail at him, she knew better. This thing between them would make or break during this conversation. Her losing control and her temper would accomplish nothing.

But she really, really wanted to yell at hime until he saw reason.

He studied her. "You're pissed."

"Correction: I'm furious."

Luca nodded. "It had to be done. I'm sorry it happened, but I'm not sorry about the outcome."

He still didn't understand. Why would he? Luca had depended on three people for the majority of his life, and they'd all learned the hard way that they couldn't trust anyone but each other. Of course he wouldn't trust Cami. She rubbed a hand over her face, suddenly exhausted. It would always be like this. He would always choose them first and mistrust everyone else's intentions.

She should have known better than to think that a week would suddenly flip a switch inside him, or that something as changeable as feelings would make a difference.

It still hurt.

"I think you should go."

Luca shook his head. "I came to apologize."

"Well, you're doing a shoddy job of it." It was too much. She couldn't keep it all inside. She wasn't even sure she wanted to anymore. "Did it ever, even once, cross your mind to ask for my help?"

His dumbfounded expression was answer enough.

She laughed, the sound hard and grating in her throat. "I didn't think so. Luca, do you really think me so heartless that I wouldn't understand what you were trying to accomplish? Whether for vengeance or because you're trying to be a modern-day superhero, it's the same result. It's a *good* thing to take down the group who steals children and puts them through what you survived. How could you think that I would set my personal aims ahead of something like *that*? Do you really think so little of me?"

His jaw worked. "You would have just agreed to throw away your freedom? Just like that. Just because I asked."

"*Yes.* Yes, you idiot, that's exactly what I would have done." It still would have hurt. She'd invested so much on this Hunt, on her chance to really put a new foot forward in her life. But it wasn't a hard decision to make, even with all that.

We protect.

"What would the price be?"

She jerked back. "What?"

Luca paced from one side of the room to the other. "Would you want me back in Thalania? Or maybe it'd be to bring the old woman here? Come on, Cami. Everyone has a price. What would mine be?"

Icy rage swept her under, so cold it hurt. "The only person thinking in those terms is you, Luca." Each word was clipped and sharp enough to cut, though from the look on his face, she was the only one bleeding out on the floor during this conversation. "Regardless, it's over now. Dolph won. Your plan is once again safe. Now, please leave."

He looked at the door and then back to her. "Did he hurt you?"

"He was the one bleeding out on the beach." And, yes, she had a back full of bruises where he'd tackled her, and he likely would have drowned her if Luca hadn't shown up when he did. She couldn't bring herself to thank him for that. Just because he wasn't the worst monster the world had to offer didn't mean he hadn't hurt her terribly.

Wasn't *still* hurting her terribly.

"Please leave. I'm not going to ask again."

For a long moment, she thought—hoped—that Luca would argue. That he'd find a reason to stay. That he'd help them navigate the treacherous waters they found themselves in. But he just nodded and moved to the door. "Goodbye, Cami."

Her legs gave out the second the door clicked shut behind him. She sank to the floor and pulled her knees to her chest. A week was only seven days. Not nearly long enough to be feeling this kind of pain over a man. Not long enough to lose her heart.

Except that was exactly what had happened.

She stared at her door for a long time, an unforgivably weak part of her willing him to come back. To actually deliver that apology he claimed to have. To promise to sit down and talk until they figured out a way forward for them.

But there was no way forward.

Luca only cared about revenge. She didn't blame him for that. In his shoes, no doubt she would feel exactly the same way. He had never promised her anything but his protection on the island. Expecting more ... She should have known better.

Cami should have known better about a lot of things.

When her self-pity became too cloying, she climbed to her feet and padded to her things. As tempting as it was to use her satellite phone for this call, she wanted them to hear. No doubt the Horsemen monitored all pertinent communication to and from the island. Let them listen to this one.

She picked up the phone and dialed slowly. If her hand shook a little, it was only to be expected. She'd *failed*. Lord, but that sucked.

As expected, Yael didn't answer her own phone. It took the assistant a few minutes to find the old woman, and then she was there, her crackling voice coming through the line. "Well?"

"I didn't win."

Silence for a beat. "Tell me."

And so she did. She told Yael about the change in the White Stag, in how Luca had entered the Wild Hunt instead. Cami left out a few pertinent sexual details, but she walked Yael through every step of the competition, through how she'd used the traps against them, and finally landed on the truths Luca had shared about his past.

Yael exhaled slowly, as if in pain. "You forfeited your win for him."

"For his goals," Cami corrected.

"For *him*."

She closed her eyes. "Yes. I forfeited my win for him."

Yael was quiet for a long time. Finally, she said, "I would have done the same thing in your place."

Cami's eyes flew open. "What?"

"You could have won. No matter what that grandson of mine thinks, you would have found a way. You chose not to. That's the important part, my girl. You *chose* not to."

"I failed."

"Did you?"

How could Yael ask that? Yael, who'd hammered her point in again and again. *Win, at all costs.* Cami had come to this island with one objective, and she hadn't accomplished it. That was the very definition of failure. "I didn't win."

"What have I told you time and time again, my girl?"

"We protect." The words felt drawn from her against her will. "But—"

"You made the right call, Camilla. It might not feel like it in this moment, but you did." A pause. "Or are you feeling poorly because you fell in love with Luca in the process?"

Cami opened her mouth, reconsidered, and shut it. "It can't be love."

"You're not a fool. Stop acting like one."

She took the phone from her ear and glared at it before replacing it. "It doesn't matter."

"Ah, that's a different thing altogether."

Damn it, but she'd hoped Yael had some sage wisdom to offer to get her out of this situation with her heart intact. Apparently that wouldn't be the case. "This is a mess."

"What will you do next?"

That was the question, wasn't it? Part of her wanted to stay, to keep fighting for ... What? Luca had his allegiance and he had his goals, and neither of them included her. She'd be a fool to think she'd even be allowed to stay on the island, let alone that it would accomplish anything.

Not to mention, she'd had no less than seventy missed calls from her brother and his two Consorts on her phone when she finally checked earlier. Hiding from *that* was a cowardly thing to do. "I'm coming home. I have to figure out what happens next, and I can't do that without facing my brother." Her king.

"Good. It's about time for me to show my face at the palace. They're getting lax in their fear of me."

Cami laughed a little. "In that case, I'll see you there."

"Goodbye, Camilla. Safe travels."

"You, too." She hung up and braced herself on the table. Going home felt like defeat, but it was the right call to make. If she couldn't magic her freedom by utilizing a favor from Death, she'd have to find a way free herself. Cami gave herself ten seconds to imagine what it would have been like to see Death and Theo go toe-to-toe and smiled. A shame it'd never happen now.

It didn't matter. She'd find a different way.

But first she had to get off this island.

Cami lifted the phone again and pressed the button for the concierge. When a man answered, she said, "I need to book a flight to Thalania, and transport to the airport on the mainland."

He didn't hesitate. "Of course, ma'am."

Cami packed in record time and turned a slow circle, looking at the room. Her gaze landed on a notepad sitting next to the bed. It was monogramed with what passed for the Horsemen's crest—a chess piece, the knight. Before she could think better of it, Cami scrawled out a quick note to Luca. She finished right as there was a knock at the door. The concierge had arrived to help her with her bags.

For better or worse, this adventure was over.

LUCA STARED at the note Cami wrote him before she left the island. He doubted it was a coincidence that the note had been delivered *after* the helicopter took off and there was no chance to convince her to stay. His siblings wanted him focused, and she was a distraction.

He read the note for the tenth time.

Happy hunting, Luca. I hope you find what you're looking for.

No matter how many times he went over the words, his brain refused to comprehend the fact that he'd underestimated her *again*, because it meant he'd made a terrible mistake. One that there was no coming back from now that she was gone. He kept picturing the way she flinched at his words, how she visibly steeled herself before cutting him off at the knees. Had he misread the situation yet again? Surely he couldn't be this fucking dense?

Luca sat up straight, letting his feet fall to the floor from their perch on his desk. "Holy shit, I fucked up."

"Glad we got that out of the way," Kenzie said as she

walked into his suite. "But you're going to have to hold off on the come to Jesus talk, because the Bookkeeper just landed, and you're going to shit yourself when you see what they look like." She flipped around a handheld monitor.

Luca blinked. "That's a woman."

"Ding, ding, ding, we have a winner!" She zoomed in as the woman walked through the halls, flanked by four guards who all wore black and gave off menacing vibes he could feel even through the screen. "Who'd have thought?"

Luca leaned in and searched this woman's face. She was a good-looking black lady, well into her fifties and carrying a strength that said she mowed down any obstacle that rose in her path and to hell with the consequences. She wore a pristine white dress that set off her dark brown skin and as she walked past the camera in the entrance, her gaze found it immediately.

"You're sure?" he asked.

"Ryu's sure." Which was as good as the same thing. Ryu might not have been able to track down their tormenters, but he wouldn't make a mistake about this.

Luca scrubbed a hand over his face. It was happening. It was finally happening. "Okay." He waited for a feeling of elation, of relief, but there was only a lingering dread. Maybe the relief would come later, once they had her in their power.

Maybe.

"Luca ..."

Whatever Kenzie had been about to say disappeared as Amarante walked into the room. "It's time." She didn't speak again until they were all gathered in the hub. Amarante met each of their gazes in turn. "The closing ceremony, such as it is, happens now. Keep your game faces on and your tempers under control—that means you, Kenzie."

"You always single me out."

"*You* always start a brawl."

Kenzie grinned, totally unrepentant. "I can't help that the Y chromosome means men have skin thin enough to shred with a sharp word."

"You can help it tonight. You will be pretty and vapid and play to their expectations. Stay in the room, stay in sight of each other."

Luca shook his head slowly. "You think she might be playing us."

"I think we can't afford to underestimate her." Amarante smoothed her hands down her tailored trousers. "We've already lost enough to them. I won't lose any more. We spin this out as planned and take her tonight."

"What if she tries to leave before then?"

Her lips pulled up into something resembling a smile. "Then she fails." Amarante checked her slim wristwatch. "It's time."

Luca fell into step next to her as they headed out of the hub and down the passageway that would take them to the party room. "What happens if she doesn't have the information we need?"

"She will."

"But—"

"She *will*." Amarante reached out, but pulled back before she touched him. "For what it's worth, I'm sorry about the princess."

Yeah, everyone seemed to be sorry about the princess. He wanted to snap back, to strike out, to blame her for the loss eating a pit in his stomach, but Luca could be honest, even in this.

He had no one to blame but himself.

He'd crossed the line with Cami, and he'd let himself get

tangled up in her. Had actively sought getting tangled up in her. Everyone around him tried to warn him off, Cami included, but he'd ignored all that and charged forward without a second thought. Even though he knew she wasn't for him, he'd wanted her all the same.

Now, he knew exactly what he was missing without her presence in his life.

A week should be too short a time to put his life on a pivot, and yet here they were. Fucking pivoting. "I don't want to let her go."

Amarante took the change of subject with ease. "Then go get her. *After* we are through with the Bookkeeper."

"It's not that simple."

She stopped in front of the door and turned to him. Behind them, Kenzie and Ryu looked on, but for once neither offered any commentary. Amarante shook her head. "Luca, since when have you ever let something as simple as social conventions get in the way of what you want? When have any of us?" She kept speaking before he could cut in, her low voice slicing to the very heart of him. "If you love her, then chase her down and convince her to give you a chance. Who gives a flying fuck about what the rest of the world thinks?"

It wasn't the rest of the world he was worried about. It was Cami. He had fucked up in her room earlier. She didn't *want* to see him. But instead of focusing on that, he took a different line. "What do *you* think?"

"It doesn't matter what I think," Amarante answered easily. "The girl isn't entirely without merit, despite what family she hails from. It's not my call, Luca. It's yours." She turned and pushed through the door, leaving the rest of them to follow in her wake.

Luca set aside his turmoil over Cami. He couldn't afford

to be distracted right now, not when walking into a room of people who'd like nothing more than to see his downfall. No one was ever happy to lose at the Wild Hunt, but this year the cold looks were particularly personal. He took up position at Amarante's left and studied the room as she started in on her short speech about the Hunt's conclusion.

The Bookkeeper sat next to Dolph, her hand casually resting on his forearm. The rest of their group sat around them, varying expressions of discontent on their faces. The next table over housed the unexpected pairing of Bellamy King and Envy. Those two exchanged a look that Luca didn't like, especially since the last time he saw Bellamy, the man had been yelling his fool head off about his sister. Desperate men made desperate deals, and Envy was just ruthless enough to take advantage of the situation.

Not my problem, he reminded himself.

Liam was the one who worried him. During the entrance events, he hadn't exactly been open or happy, but his restraint still had a relaxed element to it. Not so now. He watched everyone around him with a fury that sent alarm bells pealing through Luca's head. Those bells tripled when Liam's attention landed on Kenzie.

And stayed there.

Amarante finished speaking and polite clapping was the response. She immediately moved to congratulate the winner, but Luca caught Kenzie's arm. "Watch out for the Irishman."

Kenzie's amber eyes flicked to Liam and then away. "I've got it covered."

Oh, he didn't like that. He didn't like that at all. "We're going to talk about this."

"I said I've got it covered." She stared at his hand on her arm until he let it drop. "Smile, baby. Today is a good day."

But Luca couldn't smile. It took everything he had not to glower at anyone who came close. The minutes seemed to drip by, but all at once, he blinked and the Bookkeeper herself stood in front of him. She smiled, though the expression came nowhere near her dark eyes. "Famine."

"Ma'am."

"You know, I expected a better showing of you during these games. I have it on good authority that you're just as skilled in this area as War is."

Fury rose, a surge strong enough to steal his breath. Luca swallowed it down, though he couldn't smooth his expression. *She knew who they were.* It wasn't possible, but he couldn't shake the suspicion that her double-speak meant exactly that. "The island has a way of leveling the playing field."

"Mmm." She nodded slowly. "So does a pretty girl. How is the delightful princess? I don't see her here?" She made a show of looking around.

Every alarm bell went off in his head. "I imagine losing has a way of souring a person on parties."

"Shame. My Dolph had a few things he wanted to say to her." She shrugged. "I suppose he'll have to track her down on his own time."

Over my dead fucking body.

When Luca spoke again, he couldn't keep the growl from his voice. "It would take Death's favor for him to even get close to her."

"You underestimate our friend." The Bookkeeper smiled. "Which is a good thing, as he ceded the favor to me." She started to turn away. "I'll be seeing you, Famine."

Sooner than you realize.

Luca moved through the people slowly, resisting his urge to stalk directly to his brother, to draw attention to himself. He finally stopped next to Ryu. "Dolph doesn't leave the island."

"I thought you'd say that. The Bookkeeper is staying in his suite, so you can take care of it tonight."

Take care of it. Remove the threat.

Luca didn't *think* Dolph could get to Cami, but he wasn't willing to take the risk. He'd ensure the man never had the chance. "Good."

This was supposed to be the first in many wins.

Instead, it felt like they were under siege.

Enemies under their roof. Needing to play the roles set out for them. Danger lurking in the shadows.

The Island of Ys was supposed to be their sanctuary, their place of power. They had dangerous people there before, and he'd never felt so on edge. The Bookkeeper, while formative, was one person. Even her guards barely edged the needle in her favor. She was outgunned and outmatched, but Luca still couldn't shake the feeling of doom.

Maybe it was just him.

Maybe his doom had less to do with their plan playing out and everything to do with the new weight of loss in his chest. Luca wouldn't know. He'd never had his heart broken before. He hadn't been celibate for the entirety of his adult life by any means, but most of the time they were women visiting the island and looking for a walk on the wild side. They had no intention of pursuing something more serious, and he'd been content with that. His siblings, his revenge, mattered more than trying to figure out if a relationship was even possible.

It was different with Cami. *Cami* was different.

Luca rubbed his chest. He couldn't live like this. He

didn't *want* to live like this, bleeding out from a wound no one else could see.

He had to find a way to convince Cami to give him a chance.

A real chance.

But first ... the Bookkeeper.

And Dolph.

18

They waited for several hours after the party ended for the Bookkeeper and her people to settle in their suites. Despite what some guests thought, not every set of rooms in the island contained cameras and microphones ... But Luca and the others made damn sure that anyone worth watching ended up in a room that did.

He leaned closer to the monitor and snorted. "They brought in their own food and drink."

"Wise. I dosed all those coffee packets."

He glanced at Ryu. "That's particularly insidious."

Ryu gave a tight smile. "I know."

In the end, the human need for sleep prevailed and the Bookkeeper retreated to her private room within the suite. Luca crossed his arms over his chest. "Kenzie and I will take care of the guards and Dolph. You and Amarante handle the Bookkeeper."

Amarante nodded. "The boat is ready and so is the cell."

A little known fact about the Island of Ys. It wasn't two islands—it was three. The third was small enough not to gain notice, which was exactly how they liked it. Situated off the southwest corner of the big island, most guests never even noticed it was there. Even if they did, it looked like a thousand other islands in this part of the world—small and insignificant and, while beautiful, ultimately uninteresting.

They were wrong.

Kenzie cracked her knuckles. "Let's do this."

Adrenaline surged, burning away what was left of his malaise. He'd deal with all the other shit tomorrow. Tonight, there was only one goal.

Remove the threat.

They headed to the passageway that ran along the edge of her suite, and there they parted ways. Ryu and Amarante disappeared around a turn that would lead them to her private room. Kenzie and Luca paused outside the cleverly hidden door into the main room. They exchanged a look. "Ready?" Luca asked.

"Baby, I was born ready." She made a face when he handed her a tranq gun. "These are bad guys. I don't get why we can't just off them and be done with it. If they work for her, they are just as guilty as anyone in that association. And Dolph is *definitely* guilty of unsavory things."

Luca agreed, but this was the plan and they'd stick to it. "We use the tranquilizers. If you get bloodstains on the carpet again, Damien is liable to gut you himself." Their head of staff didn't blink at whatever they asked of him, and his loyalty was beyond question. But that didn't stop him from getting uptight about anything he viewed as fucking with his domain.

The fact that the Island of Ys belonged to the Horsemen was something he only acknowledged when he needed something from them.

Kenzie gave a put-upon sigh. "It was *one time.*"

"That's the only time I've ever heard him yell. And when

he made that sound like a pissed off teakettle? I thought we were going to have to say your last rites."

She smacked his shoulder. "Hey, now. You know damn well that *I'm* the funny one. I have the market cornered on inappropriate jokes." Kenzie grinned. "And, fine, that was a good one."

Luca glanced at the dart gun in his hands. "Dolph doesn't leave the room alive."

"Agreed." She sobered. "Let's do this."

They burst through the door in a practiced motion. Kenzie went low while Luca came in high, shooting the tranq darts before the men lounging around the room had the chance to respond. Seconds later, four of them slumped to the floor. Kenzie patted them down one by one and tsked. "These fuckers have fancy plastic guns."

"They must have hidden them in the luggage in pieces and assembled them here." He hadn't seen that in the footage, which was slightly worrisome, but in the end it didn't matter. They'd removed this threat. They could deal with the potential security risk once they were finished.

Luca stalked to where Dolph lay on the couch. The doctor who stitched up his legs had dosed him with some heavy pain meds, so Luca hadn't bothered tranqing him. The man opened his eyes as Luca leaned over him. "Famine."

"Dolph."

He gave a drugged smile. "Your girl is going to be happy to see me."

"You're never going to touch her."

Dolph snorted. "We'll see."

"No, we won't." Luca picked up the pillow on the couch and covered Dolph's face, pressing down with his full weight. It was over in a few short minutes."

Kenzie whistled. "That was too nice."

"No blood on the carpet," he reminded her. Luca tossed the pillow to the side. If he was a better person, he'd feel something resembling remorse for taking a life. He didn't. Dolph was a monster, and Luca would do worse to keep the people he cared about safe.

A knock on the door made them freeze. Kenzie waved wildly at him.

Luca raised an eyebrow. "Yes, Kenzie, I'll get the door."

"Don't you dare!" she hissed.

He strode to the door and opened it. A black man in a pair of slacks and a white button-up shirt stood there, expression impassive. Luca nodded. "Hey, Damien. We were just talking about you." He stepped back to allow the other man in, as well as the two people carting giant laundry bins. They got to work quickly, hauling the men up and into the bins and then covering them with laundry.

The Horsemen might be judge, jury, and executioner when someone stepped too far out of line on the island, but there was no reason to telegraph their intentions with this particular situation. After the staff had taken the unconscious bodies and Dolph, Damien moved through the room, studying the floor. "You managed not to damage anything. I'm impressed."

Kenzie crossed her arms over her chest and glared. "You remember who signs your checks, right?" He merely raised an eyebrow at her and she cursed. "You all are enough to drive me to drink."

Damien nodded to her and Luca, and left the room without another word. Luca rubbed a hand over his mouth. "I always liked Damien."

"Shut up." She walked to the bedroom door and opened it. Amarante and Ryu waited, a trussed-up Bookkeeper between them. The woman glared at them with an icy hatred Luca recognized, even after all this time, even without the mask hiding most of her face. Derision. As if they were dogs who had suddenly gained the ability to speak.

But then the people who owned that hell had viewed them as little more than animals. As commodities to be used and thrown away without second thought.

"The guards have been disposed of," Kenzie said.

Luca stepped forward and leaned down until his face was even with the Bookkeeper's. "Dolph will never lay a hand on anyone ever again—and neither will you."

There it was. The first sliver of fear in her dark eyes.

She finally began to understand that she'd never leave the island.

Amarante nodded. "Let's get this one to the boat." She pulled a blindfold out of her pocket and tied it around the other woman's eyes, none too gently. Then Ryu picked her up and tossed her over his shoulder. They left the same way they'd come in—through the passageways.

It was only when they reached the door to the exterior, the one that would lead them to a deserted little path on the north side of the casino and down to a dock so small, it was barely worth noticing, that Luca stopped. Ryu and Kenzie moved into the night, carefully taking the stone steps down to the dock.

Amarante stopped next to him. "You're not coming?"

"It's not really my skillset, Te." Torture wasn't his forte. He'd been the beast in the pit, the animal they dragged out when they wanted something killed and they wanted it done messy. That wasn't any use here. He wouldn't be any use in the room they had set up for the Bookkeeper. In fact, he'd be a fucking liability, because now that the adrenaline had started to fade, the gnawing in his chest was back and worse.

"No, it's mine." Her smile held no humor. "Do you know how delicious I find the irony that I'm using something *they* forced me to learn on one of their people?"

"I can imagine." They all had their issues. He hadn't lied when he told Cami that. What he hadn't told her was that Death hadn't come by her name on the island.

She'd earned it long before then.

She watched Ryu drop the Bookkeeper into the boat. "You're going after her."

"Yeah." He hesitated. "She might tell me to fuck off. I'd deserve it if she did."

"Maybe." Amarante shrugged. "Or maybe you finally found something worth fighting for that isn't tied to blood and death and our past. I won't stand in your way, Luca. I can only keep us alive. The power to make us happy lies beyond my abilities. If you have a chance ..." Now it was her turn to hesitate. "You should take it. Find your princess and make things right."

He turned to face her fully. "If things go well ... If she's willing ... I want to bring her back here, Te. No matter what Thalania thinks, my future isn't there. It's here. I think Cami's could be, too."

Amarante took him in with dark eyes. She reached out, almost hesitantly, and put her hand on his chest directly over his heart. "You don't need my blessing. But you have it all the same." She gave him a tiny push. "Go get her."

He was already moving.

Luca left the island from time to time, but never for personal reasons. He had absolutely no reason to think that Cami would want to see him, but he had to try. He'd fucked up time and time again when it came to her, but he would start making up for that immediately. She wanted her freedom? Luca would help her find a way to realize that. She didn't need Amarante's favor to make it happen.

It was only when he climbed aboard the helicopter to take him to the mainland that he registered exactly where he was headed. Thalania. The land of his birth. The place he'd intentionally avoided since the abduction. Luca closed his eyes. It didn't matter. If Cami would give him a chance, he'd fight the king himself for the right to be hers.

CAMI'S OLDEST BROTHER, the King of Thalania, met her at the airport. He wasn't alone, of course. He'd never be truly alone for the rest of his life, and watching him walk toward her with a handful of suited servicemen flanking him made her stomach clench painfully.

I don't want this life.

Theo took her hands and held them out, casting a critical eye over her. "You don't look like you were maimed or unduly injured."

"I'm fine." Except for the broken heart beating weakly in her chest, and the walls closing in around her despite standing in the spacious private hanger. "I lost."

Sympathy settled over his features. "I'm sorry." Theo actually sounded like he meant it. "I know that was important to you."

Cami wanted to snap back, to yell at him that this was exactly what he wanted—her crawling home with her tail between her legs—but she couldn't dredge up the energy. None of this was Theo's fault. Not really. He played the part laid out for him from birth, and he'd found a way to take his happiness in the mix as well. She shouldn't begrudge him that, no matter how much being home felt like someone clipped her wings.

For that week on the Island of Ys, she'd felt … Alive. Free and powerful and so wonderfully alive. Things hadn't worked out the way she planned, but *she* chose that.

Theo took her hand and placed it on her forearm, easily pivoting to fall into step next to her. "It should come as no surprise to you, but Lady Nibley decided to grace the palace with her presence earlier today. I'm assuming she's there for you since she has been ignoring every invitation I've sent for years now."

"It will be good to see Yael." It would. Her brother might try to be supportive, but Yael was one of the few people she felt truly understood her. Being able to walk through the events on the island again might help. She hoped.

Or it could drive the knife deeper into her chest with every word.

They reached the town car and Theo opened the door for her. It wasn't until they were enclosed in the backseat that he spoke again. "I really am sorry, Cami."

"I know."

He sighed and slouched back against the seat. "I know you're looking for something, and we'll figure it out. I want you happy. I have that. Even Edward has that. You deserve it, too."

"You have a love match with *two* of the people you care most about in the world. You can't pretend that the public would allow another Fitzcharles to make the same call."

He clenched his jaw. "I stand by what I said, Cami. You can be pissed at me for breaking that mold if you need to, but I try really fucking hard not to be a hypocrite."

She knew that. Of course she knew that. Theo wouldn't try to stand in her way, no matter what she did. She couldn't even pretend to paint him as the jerky overbearing brother. It wasn't his fault that Cami felt crushed by the weight of expectation. Edward had married a noble and that union restored some of the goodwill that Theo's marriage to Galen and Meg had tarnished. It stood to reason that her following in the same footsteps would stabilize things further. No matter that Theo said he would support her, she knew he hoped that she'd make the safe choice of falling in love with a suitable candidate.

The irony that Luca *would* have been a suitable candidate was not lost on her, though she had a feeling Theo wouldn't appreciate it.

The drive to the palace passed mostly in silence. She could tell he wanted to say something to fix this, but for once her big brother had no idea how to mend the situation. Cami wasn't much help. *She* didn't know how to move forward, either. All she could think about was the island and what happened there. About how much it hurt to leave.

She made the right call. She had no illusions about that, especially after her conversation with Luca went so sideways. No matter how she felt about him, he was just like so many other people in her life—they wanted to put her in a safe little box and expected her to stay there and be content.

Cami didn't want to be protected. She could protect herself.

She wanted someone who'd trust her to fight at their side as equals.

Being back in the palace felt like voluntarily entering a gilded cage. It was beautiful and perfect and practically glowed ... and she hated it.

Theo walked her to her rooms and hesitated. "I'm here if you need me, Cami. I'm serious."

"I know." And she did. Theo would move heaven and

earth for those he loved. As king, he actually had the power to make things most people considered impossible happen. Since Cami couldn't quite put her finger on what she actually wanted, what course of action her path should take, she couldn't ask Theo for help. Not yet. It would be like renting out a wrecking ball before you knew what you wanted to demolish.

"Meg and Galen would like to see you. How about dinner later?"

"She has plans."

They both turned as Yael, Lady Nibley, walked up. She leaned more heavily on her cane than she had last time Cami saw her, but she was still moving of her own power. Cami didn't miss the two attendants hovering just out of reach, though. No doubt one of them was a doctor who would administer help as needed. Yael was never without one anymore.

Cami moved to her and pressed two quick kisses to her wrinkled cheeks. "It's good to see you."

"You, too. You, too." She turned a hawkish look on Theo. "Is it customary for the king to keep the royal princess lingering in the hallways?"

Theo didn't quite curse in exasperation, but he looked like he wanted to. "Of course not. Cami, I'm glad you're home. We'll set up something soon." He turned and stalked away, his striding eating up the distance until he turned the corner and disappeared.

Cami turned back to Yael. "Would you like to come in?"

"No, girl, I want to stand out in the hallway and gossip where anyone can hear."

Cami rolled her eyes. She should have known better than to ask a stupid question. She opened the door and let Yael precede her into the suite. It smelled just as fresh as when she'd left it, despite her avoiding the palace more and more over the years. They sank onto the couch in the sitting room and Yael took her hands. "You shouldn't have come back."

"Yael—"

"If you're in a cage, it's of your own making. Do you think Theodore would hunt you to the ends of the earth if you told him you'd be happier somewhere else?"

Theo was more than capable of it, but she didn't think for a second he'd do something that would actively harm her if she communicated her needs. That was the problem, though. Cami didn't *know* what she needed. Something not here, something unattainable.

Something connected to the Island of Ys.

She looked at her hands clasped in her lap. "He won't come back."

Yael took the change of subject in stride. "I gathered that after the third delegation we sent returned without him. For better or worse, my grandson knows his own mind." She chuckled. "It runs in the family."

That it did. But Cami couldn't leave things there. "The whole thing—the Wild Hunt, the guest list, everything— this year was a bait to draw in someone they've attempted to track down for a long time."

"They'll use him to find the others."

"Yes."

Yael studied the large ruby at the top of her cane. "Purpose. Exactly what you've been missing this entire time."

That was exactly it. *Purpose.* The chance to contribute to the greater good in a truly meaningful way instead of posing for pictures and doing charity work that, while useful, was not Cami's strength. It was all too passive, too constrained.

What she'd had on the island, what they accomplished there ... It was neither. "It doesn't matter."

"That's a defeatist attitude. I taught you better."

She sighed. "I'm sorry. You're right. I'm just feeling morose and it's making me dramatic."

Yael tapped her cane a few times, and finally said. "More happened on that island than you've told me. Was it my boy?"

Cami pictured the expression on Luca's face at being called "my boy" and smiled. "He's something else."

"Tell me everything."

This time, she did.

19

Luca weighed several different plans of action during the flight to Thalania. They were all bad. It might have been different if Cami was in one of the country estates, but when he landed, Ryu confirmed that the king himself had transported her to the palace. Luca was good, but even he couldn't sneak into the Thalanian palace without some serious preparation and time. He didn't have the luxury of either.

He couldn't shake the belief that if he didn't make things right *now*, he'd never get another chance. Cami was somewhere within those walls, and he'd move heaven and earth to get to her. If *she* turned him away ...

Well, he'd deal with that when he got there.

After about thirty seconds of consideration, he said to hell with it and walked up to the guard station at the gate. The white man was in his thirties and fit, and he gave Luca a suspicious once-over. "Can I help you?"

"I'm here to see Princess Camilla."

"You and every other jerk-off around here." The guy shook his head. "Yeah, mate, that's not going to happen."

Damn it, he didn't want to do this. Words had meaning, no matter what the intent was behind them. If he claimed his heritage now, he couldn't go back. Luca glanced at the palace. It was *so fucking close*. He swallowed against his suddenly dry throat. "I'm Lady Nibley's grandson."

The man looked at him, and then looked at him again. He pointed to a spot a few feet away. "Wait there."

Luca obediently walked to the indicated spot, even though all he wanted to do was rush the gates. So close ...

He wouldn't get a chance to talk to Cami if he was in the dungeon or whatever the hell they had in this place for prisoners. Luca knew security—he'd handled it enough on the island—and the palace's seemed to be above reproach. There were cameras all over the place, and in the fifteen minutes he stood there, guards passed by in pairs several times. *Lot of security.*

But then, he'd heard that the lady Consort had just recently had another baby. After the trouble they had when the king took the throne—*re*took the throne—it stood to reason that he and the male Consort would be overprotective. They had ... He couldn't remember. A couple kids now.

Plenty of people between Cami and the throne.

A pair of men walked through the gate. One of was a giant fucker who had to be nearly seven feet tall and had a nasty scar around his throat where someone apparently tried to cut his head off. The other was closer to Luca's height, though his expression said *he* was the dangerous one.

He was the one who looked Luca over. "Isaac, search him."

Luca held still as the giant patted him down none too gently. Only when the guy backed up did the first one nod. "Let's go."

He opened his mouth to ask questions, but ultimately decided against it. They were taking him through the gates and into the palace. That was what he wanted ... Even if Luca didn't like the way either of them looked at him. He thought he could take one of them in a fight. Both? He was good, but he wasn't convinced he was *that* good. Especially with his injured shoulder. *This is what I get for rushing in here without a goddamn plan.*

They led him in through a side door and down several hallways to a room that gave all appearances of being a sitting room. The furniture was all dainty and feminine, and Luca moved deeper into the room. No telling if the palace had passageways the same way the casinos on the island did, but he couldn't afford to assume it didn't. Finally, he took up a spot near a pretty chair he could break with one hit and use as a weapon.

The mountain of a man stood next to the door and crossed his arms over his massive chest. The other paced slowly back and forth, never taking his attention from Luca.

After two minutes of that bullshit, Luca finally said, "As fun as this has been, I was telling the truth about who I am."

"I know," the pacing man said. "You think we sent *three* fucking delegations to that island of yours without knowing who you are and what you look like? Give us a little fucking credit, Luca." He practically snarled the last word. "Or is it Famine?"

"Luca is fine," he said, trying to hold onto his temper. This man might grate him in way that made him want to beat the fucker's face in, but he couldn't afford to lose his temper.

The man stopped short. "You said you were here for Cami. What the fuck do you want with her?"

"That's between me and the princess." Who was this guy

to her? Not her brother, the king. Luca hadn't met with the delegations, had purposefully been in a different part of the island each time someone from Thalania was sent to convince him to come back, but he knew what Theodore looked like. This wasn't him.

"Wrong. That's between you and three other people before you ever get to her."

He was so over this shit. Luca stared the guy down. "Unless you're planning on tossing me in some dungeon, get the fuck out of my way."

"We don't have a dungeon," the giant said. "Haven't for ages."

Luca ignored the man and focused on the other one. "I'm waiting."

The door opened and a third man stepped in. One look at him confirmed that *this* was, in fact, King Theodore Fitzcharles III. He had the same coloring as Cami, though his eyes were dark where hers were blue, and he carried himself as if the entire world held its breath at his whim. Power. A whole shit ton of power, and comfortable with it, too. He gave the angry one a mild look. "Are you threatening one of the peers of the realm, Galen?"

Galen. As in Consort Galen, one third of the Royal Triad. Head of security and husband to the king.

Luca studied him with new interest. This was Cami's brother-in-law, which meant he was family. *Fuck me.*

Galen snorted. "He's here for Cami."

Theo turned back to Luca. "My little sister came home hurting, and it's not solely because she lost the Wild Hunt. Are you to blame?"

He could deny it until he was blue in the face, but Luca would rather fight it out in an honest battle than try to lie.

"We had a misunderstanding, and she left before I could make it right. I'm here to do that now."

"I see." Which could mean anything or nothing.

"You can't honestly plan to let him talk to her," Galen growled. "Look at this asshole. If he hurt Cami, then I don't give a fuck what Lady Nibley will say, he needs to be sent back to that little shithole of an island he loves so much."

"Galen." Just the man's name in that same mild tone, nothing more. Theo sank into the chair across from Luca with a careless grace. "Let's put it all out on the table, shall we?"

Luca reluctantly sank into the tiny chair he'd previously considered using for a weapon. That path was lost to him now. Even if he could fight his way free, touching the monarch of a country would paint the kind of target on his forehead that no one wanted to deal with. If the glowering Galen didn't kill him, Amarante sure as fuck would for being such an idiot.

Theo didn't appear to need an answer. "You and your people have turned us away every time we've sought reconciliation in the last few years. You've shown no interest in claiming your heritage, despite some rather aggressive tactics on your grandmother's part. Until now."

"Until now," Luca echoed. There wasn't a question in there, and he refused to offer information unnecessarily. He was here for Cami, not to draw Thalania into the Horsemen's plans.

Theo looked at him for what felt like a small eternity, though it was likely only a few seconds. "Is this some deeper game or are your intentions pure?"

"I'm here for Cami," Luca repeated for the millionth fucking time. "Nothing and no one else."

"We'll see." Theo motioned to the giant. "Isaac will take

you to an appropriate room. If my sister wants to see you, then she'll see you."

"And if she doesn't."

Theo raised a brow. The expression was identical to the one Cami wore when she thought he'd asked a stupid question. "Then we'll see," Theo repeated.

That answered that. If Cami didn't want to see him, they'd kick his ass to the curb. Luca wanted to argue further, but in the end his best bet lay with following orders and hoping Cami was willing to see him.

If she wasn't …

He didn't know what he'd do if she didn't want to see him. A dark voice whispered that it was nothing more than he deserved. He was tarnished goods, and she was pure in a way that had nothing to do with being shiny and new and innocent. She was just *good*, and he was most assuredly not. Maybe he deserved her turning him away. How selfish of him to want to drag her down into the dark just because he loved her.

Every time the word crossed his mind, it felt new and surprising and terrifying. He'd known it for the truth back on the island, even before she'd demanded he help her haul Dolph's unconscious body to the extraction point.

Her choice. Always her choice.

Luca hesitated by the door and looked back at the king and Consort. "I don't deserve her. I know that better than you do. But I don't give a fuck, because I'm willing to fight for her and I'll give every last piece of me to make sure she's happy for the rest of her life."

Galen's brows dropped, but Theo's expression didn't change. "Don't tell me that. Tell her."

And then there was nothing left to say.

CAMI WALKED into the throne room, and stopped. What was going on? Theo liked to keep his interactions with family informal, but now he sat in the throne up on the dais, his elbows braced on his thighs, his hands clasped loosely between his knees. Standing on either side of him were his Consorts, Meg and Galen.

The door shut behind her with an ominous click, leaving her to walk alone across the room the spot where supplicants stood at the bottom of the steps. "You called for me ... Your Highness." She could count on one hand how many times she called Theo by his royal title and still have fingers left over, but Cami couldn't read this situation so she erred on the side of caution.

"It's come to my attention that you're not happy here."

Yes, because she told him herself many times over the last few years. That fact had never earned a formal audience before. "Yes, Your Highness."

His mouth twisted. "Let's leave off the titles, Cami. You're not in trouble, and there's no one here to impress but us." Over his shoulder, Meg gave what was probably a reassuring smile, but Cami couldn't focus on anything but her brother. Theo leaned back. "You're not happy. You disobeyed a direct order to return to Thalania instead of participating in the Wild Hunt that they host on the Island of Ys. You put yourself in danger and, by extension, you put Thalania in danger."

She wished she could say this was just Theo being dramatic, but he was right. Cami's position as princess meant she made an ideal hostage if someone was so inclined. It hit particularly close to home for her brother because *Meg* was taken hostage during the time directly after she'd been established as a Consort. Cami wasn't sure either Theo or Galen had ever gotten over the fear of her being hurt after that. It ramped their already overbearing protectiveness up to an eleven and left it there.

And Cami had willfully ignored all of it. "I know."

He sighed. "We have a decision to make, little sister, and unfortunately I can't step in and make the choice one way or another. It has to be you."

She blinked. "I don't understand."

"Your role as princess is shackling you. You want freedom, you've said it often enough and I imagine that's still the case considering your recent actions."

"Yes," she said slowly.

"Your choices are this—reign yourself in, stop fighting me every step of the way and start to do Thalania's bidding ... or be disinherited."

The breath rushed from her body. "What?" She looked at Meg and then Galen. Neither of them gave her anything to work with. "*What?*" she repeated.

"You're my sister, Cami. You'll always be my sister, and you'll always be welcome here, both as family and as a citizen of Thalania, but I can't have you acting the part of a wild cannon while you're still in line for the throne, no matter how far down the line."

The rushing in her ears got loud. "You're such a bastard." How was she supposed to choose? What was she supposed to *do* if she wasn't Princess Camilla Fitzcharles? Her skillset wasn't suited for civilian life. Oh, she was young enough to get a degree and figure it out, but that didn't explain why Theo was doing this *now* and so formally.

"Hold that verdict for a moment." He nodded at Galen. "There's someone I want you to talk to before you make your decision."

If anything, Galen's glare gained an edge. He cursed and stalked down to her. "For the record, I don't agree with this."

"Thank you."

"Don't thank me, Cami. I should whoop your ass for pulling that stunt with the Wild Hunt. You could have been killed." He didn't pause long enough for her to generate a response, heading toward one of the side doors leading off the throne room. They were smaller, slightly more informal rooms for meetings that Theo wanted an official edge to, but didn't want to conduct in the grand hall itself. *Wish I'd been so lucky.* It stung. The whole situation stung.

Theo was threatening to *disinherit* her?

She didn't want the throne. She'd made that more than abundantly clear. But it was just one more blow in the line of so many she'd received lately. Her whole identity was wrapped up in being a princess. Maybe if …

But no. She couldn't afford to think like that.

Galen shoved open the door and stepped back. "Take as much time as you need." He waited for her to walk into the room and then all but slammed the door behind her.

Cami blinked in the lower light, her eyes trying to adjust. When she realized she wasn't alone, realized *who* was in this room with her, her knees buckled and her heart tried to beat out of her chest. "Luca? What are you doing here?"

20

Luca crossed the distance between them in two long strides, putting their bodies almost kissably close. But he didn't touch Cami, didn't make any move to remove the last bit of space between them. "You left without saying goodbye."

She blinked, blinked again. "You came to Thalania to … say goodbye?"

He huffed out something resembling a laugh and raked his hand through his hair. "No. Though now that I'm seeing you again, I don't even know what the fuck to say." He let his hand drop. "We got the Bookkeeper."

"Oh. Well." What was happening? She pressed her lips together, barely daring to hope. "That's good." Even knowing this might not be what she wanted, she couldn't help drinking in the sight of him. He wore a suit like the one he'd had on when they first met, though the scruff on his face now edged toward an actual beard. What caught and held her, though, was the circles under his eyes. "Have you slept at all since I saw you?"

"No." Just that. Nothing more.

Lord, but she might actually strangle this man. Cami took a careful breath. "Luca ... Why are you here? You told me you'd never come to Thalania. Not for any reason."

"Yeah, well, I hadn't fallen for you yet." He looked away and back at her, as if he couldn't bear *not* to look at her. "I've never done this, Cami. There were exactly three people I cared about in this world up to this point, and it's different than how I feel about you. Amarante, Kenzie, and Ryu are my siblings in arms. When I worry about them, it's secondary to trusting that they can handle their shit because we have a couple decades under our belt of doing exactly that."

Where was he going with this? "Okay," she said slowly.

He huffed out a breath. "I'm fucking this up. Let me start over." Luca paced away and then back to her. "I love you, Cami. I love you and it scares the shit out of me because I've never cared about *anything* the way I care about you. It makes me act like a fucking idiot even when I know damn well that you can take care of yourself. You're strong and capable and the sexiest woman I've ever met. I don't deserve you. I know that, and you know that. But if you give me a chance, I'll spend the rest of my life fighting for you, fighting to be the man you *do* deserve."

She swayed a little, his words washing over her in a rush. He ... He ... Cami swallowed hard and tried to *think*, but the only word her mind seemed to be capable of was *yesyesyesyesyesyesyes*. She cleared her throat. "You didn't trust me to handle myself on the island."

"I was fucking terrified that something would happen to you and it made me an idiot." He made a face. "I can't promise I won't be an idiot in the future."

"You want ... What are you asking me, Luca?"

"Come back to the island with me. Take up our fight."

He gave a small smile. "Eventually, when it's the right time for us, say yes when I propose to you. Later, maybe babies or some shit. We can open the subject for negotiation when we're both ready."

Take up the fight. Marriage. Babies.

Cami pressed her hand to her mouth. *Now* she understood what Theo was doing with that ultimatum in the throne room. He was setting her free. The old saying about a man not being able to serve two masters never applied more than when it concerned royalty. If he disinherited her, her actions would no longer reflect Thalania as a whole the same way they did now. She *could* fight with Luca and the other Horsemen.

She could make a difference in this world.

Cami looked up into Luca's dark eyes. *I could spend the rest of my life with this man.* "I love you, too, you know."

"I'd hoped." He reached out almost hesitantly and cupped her jaw, lowering down until he pressed his forehead against hers. "Come back to the island, Cami. Be mine. Let me be yours. It won't be easy, and sometimes it might be downright dangerous, but you'll be free."

"And I'll be with you."

She felt his smile. "And you'll be with me."

She tilted her head back and found his lips. The first brushing was almost tentative, but then she nipped his bottom lip hard enough to sting, and he growled. "Your brother is right out that door. He might be willing to give me the benefit of the doubt, but his Consort isn't."

Ah. Yes. Galen. He really would kick their asses if she let things get out of control right now. Though she was tempted to point out how hypocritical that was—Galen and Meg and Theo had tarnished *many* a sitting room in the palace over the years—there was still the matter of her disinheritance to deal with.

Cami stepped back, but claimed Luca's hand. She still couldn't quite wrap her mind around the fact this was happening, but she wouldn't let him go in the meantime while reality settled in. She opened the door ... and nearly ran into Galen. Cami glared. "You were eavesdropping."

"Safety precaution." He aimed a deadly glare over her head at Luca, but turned and headed back to his place at Theo's right hand.

"I fucking hate that guy," Luca muttered under his breath.

She laughed. She couldn't help it. Cami tugged Luca with her to the same spot she'd occupied just a few short minutes ago. "I've made a decision."

A bittersweet smile pulled at Theo's mouth. "I see that you have."

"Please disinherit me, brother. I'm going back to the island."

He nodded. "Consider it done." Theo rose gracefully and walked down the stairs to pull her into a tight hug. "No matter what, you always have a place here if you need it, and you'll always be my sister." He pressed a quick kiss to her forehead. "I love you, Cami, and I'm proud of you."

"I love you, too."

He stepped back and focused on Luca. "I respect that you want nothing to do with your heritage, but you might consider seeing your grandmother before you leave."

And then Meg was there, sweeping Cami into a tight hug that stole her breath. "You have to come back regularly and see your nieces and nephews—and *me*."

"I will. I promise I will." This was happening. It was really happening.

Meg released her and moved back, and then Galen was there, still glaring. He finally sighed. "You know I argued against this."

Cami laughed a little. "I figured."

He finally gave a reluctant smile. "You were brilliant in the Wild Hunt." He shook his head when her jaw dropped. "Did you really think we wouldn't watch? I'm proud of you, too." He gave her a rough, slightly awkward hug and then turned to Luca. "If anything happens to her, it's your head."

"Noted."

And, just like that, Cami ceased to be a princess of Thalania.

LUCA COULDN'T REMEMBER the last time he'd been this nervous. Except, yes he could, because it happened earlier that day when he stood in that small room and waited for Cami to walk through the door, not knowing which way things would play out. Now here he was, waiting alone again.

He checked his phone. Cami had said she'd be right back, but that was twenty minutes ago. Luca didn't like his chances if he tried to wander the halls looking for her.

Damn it, she said wait. So he'd wait.

The door opened and Cami walked through, an old woman on her arm. Luca stood slowly, his emotions a tangled mess inside him. This woman ... Yael. His grand-mother. He planted his feet and forced himself to breathe.

Luca had told himself any number of things in the last fifteen-odd years when it came to Yael and Thalania. That he didn't care what she thought of him. That he hated her and the country for letting him slip through their fingers. That he never wanted to see her again.

A lie. All of it.

Cami released her arm and took several steps back, though her body was tensed as if she thought Yael might collapse. If she was sick, he saw no evidence of it. Just decades upon decades' worth of living. Her white hair was a close-cropped cloud around her head and her face and neck and hands were wrinkled marked with age.

She was beautiful.

He went to his knees before her without having any intention of doing so. "Yael."

She stared down her rather large nose at him and shifted her grip on the cane in one gnarled hand. "Whether you were gone a day or twenty years, I'm still your grandmother, boy." She pressed her thin lips together and gave her head a short shake. "I never thought to see you again."

"I'm sorry." To his surprise, he actually meant it. He might want nothing to do with this country or his so-called legacy and family, but this woman had marked his first ten years the same way Amarante had marked the last seventeen. Luca reached out tentatively and took her free hand in both of his. There was strength there, despite everything, and he recognized it down to his very soul. "I owe my survival to the family I chose but ... I wouldn't have lasted long enough to find them if you weren't my grandmother." If she hadn't passed that immeasurable strength down to him. He could admit that now, even if he had never been able to before.

"Oh, my boy. My beautiful, beautiful boy." She squeezed his hand, hers shaking. "You have nothing to apologize for. If wasn't you who failed. It was *me*." She cleared her throat. "But it's something neither of us can take back, no matter how much we'd like to. In the end, you did more than survive." She gave him a tight smile. "I'm proud of you, Luca."

He never thought he'd need to hear those words, but they struck right to the core of him. "Would you like to see my home?"

Her smile widened a little. "I've only got another year left in me, less than that if the doctors are to be believed. It seems fitting that my last trip will be to that island of yours." She raised white brows. "Little melodramatic to pick that particular myth for inspiration, don't you think?"

"My sister has a strange sort of sense of humor."

The wrinkles on her face deepened with her smile. "I'd like to meet this girl, too. Both of them, and that brother of yours." She glanced at Cami, who stood watching with shining eyes. "You take care of my boy, you hear? I had a feeling when you were children that you'd be well suited. It's fitting how these things turn out."

"Very fitting," Cami said with a wobble in her voice.

"No tears, my girl. This is a happy time." She tugged on Luca's hands. "Off your knees. You're a sovereign nation, and that means you kneel to no one." She reached out and Cami was immediately there, allowing Yael to join their two hands. "I can die in peace now."

"Yael!" Cami glared. "Don't you dare talk like that."

"I'm not ready to go quite yet." She laughed drily. "But I'll have no regrets when I do." She looked up into Luca's face, and he couldn't begin to guess what she saw there. Yael nodded. "No doubt you'll be jetting off as soon as possible. Expect me on the island within a month."

"Yes, ma'am." When she narrowed her eyes, he quickly amended. "Yes, Grandmother."

Yael gave him one last smile and walked out of the room,

seeming stronger than when she'd first entered. Cami shuddered out a sigh. "I'm not ready for her to be gone."

"Me, either." He could rage against the wasted years, but in the end they had right now. He pulled Cami into his arms and rested his chin on the top of her head. "That was both more difficult and infinitely easier than I expected."

"She's something else." He could hear the smile in her voice.

"Yes, she really, really is." He exhaled. "Come home with me, Cami. The fight's just beginning and I wouldn't have anyone at my side but you."

She squeezed him hard. "I'm there. I'll always be there."

ON THE SMALLEST island owned by the Four Horsemen, Amarante finished her work. She turned her back on the woman slumped in the chair and met her brother's gaze. Ryu sighed. "Three names isn't much."

"It's a thread to pull." She moved to the sink positioned just inside the door. She could feel the Bookkeeper's blood seeping through her pores, infecting her with the woman's particular brand of evil.

Or Amarante would if she believed in that sort of thing.

Evil was real. It stalked through the world in a thousand different forms, all carrying the same selfish desire that cared little for who it hurt in the process. Most people simply didn't act it on the scale of the Bookkeeper and the people who paid her.

Amarante cleaned her hands and forearms with steady motions. Her hands didn't shake. She mourned that loss of human reaction silently, another thing the people in Camp Bueller had taken from her.

Another thing she'd never reclaim.

Ryu moved to stand beside her. "I can handle the rest."

"You don't have to shield me." Neither Kenzie nor Luca would have even thought to offer. They saw her strength as unparalleled, without the slightest weakness. They would simply take her words at face value.

Not Ryu, though.

But then, he had a lifetime of knowing her to fall back, and there was a time when Amarante wasn't Death. When she was just a girl with a little brother who thought the sun rose and set with her.

It was so long ago.

Ryu shook his head. "I can handle the rest," he repeated.

She bit back her instinctive response to power through simply because that's what she'd always done. Not this time. She wasn't alone. She wasn't even the glue keeping their foursome together anymore. The foundations were too strong to be held by a single person. Amarante simply said, "Thank you."

Three names.

Not as much as she'd hoped for, but it would be enough.

It *had* to be enough.

She pushed through the door and found Kenzie leaning against the wall. She looked up. "It's done?"

"Yes." Amarante carefully closed the door behind her, standing between Kenzie and the scene in the room she'd just left. "It's time to go hunting."

THANK you so much for reading Luca and Cami's story! This was a departure for me in a number of ways, I enjoyed the hell out of writing it. I hope the wild ride was a great one for you!

The Horsemen's story isn't over! The series picks up directly after the end of HIS FORBIDDEN DESIRE with HER RIVAL'S TOUCH. Kenzie is going to have to deal with the fact that Liam is on the island—and he's there for HER. What's a woman to do in that situation? A bet sounds about right...

Want to ensure you never miss a new release or a sale? Make sure to sign up for my newsletter! Newsletter subscribers also get exclusive content every month, including teasers, cover reveals, and exclusive short stories.

Want to know more about how Cami's older brother, Theo, found his two Consorts and retook the throne after he was exiled? You can pick up THEIRS FOR THE NIGHT, my FREE novella that goes back to where the Royal Triad first began. An exiled prince, his bodyguard, and the bartender they can't quite manage to leave alone.

READ a sneak peek of HER RIVAL'S TOUCH now!

LIAM HAD KNOWN the truth even before he saw it reflected in Kenzie's hazel eyes. She had no memory of him. None. The night eight years ago might have been imprinted beneath his skin, but she'd walked and never spared him a second thought. Fuck, he was an idiot.

It didn't change his reason for being here.

He might have entered the Wild Hunt with the intention of securing Death's favor to find the woman who haunted his dreams all these years, but he honestly hadn't expected to arrive on the island and see *her*. What were the odds? Too impossible to put a number to.

And yet here she was.

She flipped her blond hair off her shoulder and glared up at him. "What are you on about?"

"Boston. Eight years ago. We shared a bottle of top shelf whiskey in a little hole in the wall bar and then fucked on every surface of your hotel room. And then you robbed me."

She looked at him as if seeing him for the first time, and he found himself holding his breath while he waited. That flicker of recognition in her hazel eyes died. "Sorry, you've got the wrong girl."

She does *remember me.*

He fucking *knew it.*

"No, I don't." He leaned forward. He couldn't help himself. The siren call of her was too much to deny. Liam lowered his voice and delivered his knockout punch. "Kenzie."

She jerked as if he'd hooked her up to a live wire. "How do you know that name?"

It proved his theory that she didn't just randomly give out her name to people—publicly she was known as War and only that—which, in turn, supported the fact that that night had meant as much to her as it had to him. "You told me." He should have left it there, but frustration boiled beneath his skin, a product of too many days spent inactive, within touching distance of his goal but unable to close the distance. "While you were riding my cock for the third time."

She paled, but recovered almost instantly and cast a look at the front of his slacks. "Maybe if I saw your cock, I'd actually remember you."

Stupid to let the cut land. He'd known that it wouldn't be

easy to find the mystery woman, let alone to convince her to give him a shot. She had all the information she needed in the wallet she'd stolen from him. If she wanted to find him after that, she could have.

"A conversation, Kenzie."

"Stop saying that name," she hissed.

"A conversation," he repeated. "Surely that's not too much to ask."

She frowned. "A conversation and then you leave."

"Sure," he lied easily. Now that he'd found her, he wasn't leaving until he saw this through one way or another. His best friend, Aiden, had called him an idiot for hunting the idea of a woman he'd met once, but that night was a fever in his blood that he couldn't ease. He needed to know if there was something there, or at least get some fucking closure so he could move on with his life. There had never been time for selfish pursuits, not when the O'Malley family teetered on the verge of war and needed every solider on alert. Now there was finally peace, which meant now he was free to pursue his dream.

To pursue Kenzie.

She finally shrugged. "Fine. I can spare five minutes."

Fuck, but this woman was harder to pin down than smoke. Even when he'd failed to win the Wild Hunt, he hadn't lost hope because now he knew where she was. Except he couldn't get to her. Every time he caught sight of her blond wave of hair, or the red she seemed to wear like a banner of war, she'd disappear just as fast. This place had to be riddled with back doors and hallways the public didn't know about, because he'd never had someone slip his grasp so many times. The frustration had him going out of his skin.

He followed her through the cascade of sound the slot

machines emitted. It was wasn't smoky in here like in some casinos, and the air had the faintest tinge of salt as a reminder that they weren't far from the water. A temptation to leave the four walls of this place and walk outside. Liam shook it off. He wasn't there for the same reason the other patrons were.

He was there for Kenzie.

Pre-order HER RIVAL'S TOUCH now!

ACKNOWLEDGMENTS

Huge thanks to all my readers for taking this leap with me. The Island of Ys has been kicking around in the back of my brain for a long time, and it's really satisfying to be able to bring some of those wayward side characters forward to get their own HEAs!

Big thank you to Eagle and Lynda for helping me make this book the best version of itself.

Thank you, as always, to my ladies. Piper and Asa and Lauren for always being there to help talk me through snags and share in the ups and downs and unexpected pivots!

Last, but never least, thank you to Tim. It's been a wild ride and it doesn't show any signs of slowing down anytime soon. I love you like a love song, babe!

ABOUT THE AUTHOR

New York Times and USA TODAY bestselling author Katee Robert learned to tell her stories at her grandpa's knee. Her 2015 title, The Marriage Contract, was a RITA finalist, and RT Book Reviews named it 'a compulsively readable book with just the right amount of suspense and tension." When not writing sexy contemporary and romantic suspense, she spends her time playing imaginary games with her children, driving her husband batty with what-if questions, and planning for the inevitable zombie apocalypse.

www.kateerobert.com

Keep up to date on all new release and sale info by joining Katee's NEWSLETTER!